Because Desert<

Igor Kaczurowsky

Because Deserters Are Immortal

Translated from the Ukrainian
by Yuri Tkacz

Bayda Books
Melbourne 2022

First published in Australia in 1979.
Second revised edition 2022

Bayda Books
P.O. Box 178
East Brunswick VIC 3057 Australia
Email: ytkacz@gmail.com

"Because Deserters Are Immortal" was original published in
Ukrainian in Germany in 1956 as *Shliakh nevidomoho*.
Ukrainian copyright © Igor Kaczurowskyj, 1956
English translation copyright © Yuri Tkacz 1979, 2022

Cover art by Olga Kohut
Artistic design – Anton Tkacz

FICTION
ISBN 979 8 842991 04 4

CONTENTS

TRANSLATOR'S PREFACE

Igor Kaczurowsky (1918-2013) was born in Nizhyn, Ukraine. His father was a civil servant, while his mother came from the landed gentry. Because of his mother's social background, the family was persecuted and had to move to Kursk in Russia to avoid arrest. There Igor obtained his education. In 1942, with the arrival of the Germans, the family returned to their native town. However, with the collapse of the German front in 1943, they fled west to Austria, later emigrating to Argentina in 1948, where they settled in the slums of Buenos Aires. The next twenty years Igor worked as a labourer.

By the end of the 1950s he had learnt Spanish and had become a part-time lecturer at the Salvador University in Buenos Aires. After marrying, he moved to Munich where he worked for Radio Liberty.

Igor began publishing poetry in 1946, and his first collection in 1948 was highly acclaimed. There followed six more collections. His three books of literary prose include this book and its sequel *The House on the Cliff* (1966), and *The Iron Kulak* (1959, 2005).

The author also translated many poets into Ukrainian and published six scholarly works on various aspects of Ukrainian literature. Kaczurowsky has also penned several hundred articles and papers on literary subjects. Many of his books were republished in Ukraine after it achieved independence in 1991. In 2006 he was awarded the prestigious Shevchenko Prize for literature.

Because Deserters are Immortal features episodes from the life of a young Ukrainian intellectual who during World War 2 finds himself between the millstones of two demonic dictatorships – those of Stalin and Hitler. In her review of the book Caroline Edgerton draws attention to the novel's anti-existential motifs.

Igor Kaczurowsky is acclaimed worldwide – both in the Ukrainian diaspora and in Ukraine proper as an eminent poet, translator, and scholar.

I am indebted to the author for his help in providing information for the footnotes. Also, my sincere thanks to everyone who made this book possible, especially Graham Hirst for his painstaking

editing of the manuscript. For this second revised edition, a big thank you to my son Anton, who learnt how to navigate the intricacies of publishing on the Amazon platform.
Yuri Tkacz

DESERTERS

An intensive purge of the Party was under way throughout the whole country, so it was not surprising that I also took part and helped several of my friends to purge themselves. This purge differed greatly from previous ones: this time Party and Komsomol[1] members were purging themselves, occasionally with the help of their most trusted friends, burying or burning their Party cards, and in their 'military card' scratching out the dangerous words 'Member of the CPSU(B)[2] (or Komsomol)' and substituting them with 'non-party person'. My neighbour on the left had just brought me two 'cards' to purge – his own and that of a friend, for whose reliability he vouched. I should explain that this was the autumn of 1941, when even the adherents of Bolshevism began to persuade themselves that they were its opponents and when the general attitude toward the war flowed in a simple and clear formula, expressed simultaneously by millions of different people in all corners of the country: 'We've lost the war'.

Beyond all doubt, war begins for each person when he first learns of it. For the border units of the Soviet Army the war began in the early hours of 22 June; for the rest of the Soviet Union's population, it began in the afternoon of 22 June after the news was announced on the radio. For the Siberian backwoodsman who didn't listen to the radio or read the newspapers, it began two to three weeks later, when the news arrived on foot. For me personally the war began on... 30 April, for that was the day I learned that war with the Germans had been finally decided.

Immediately I began taking defensive action. Although I already had a 'clean ticket', just to be certain I developed diseased lungs, heart and liver conditions attested to by real, genuine doctors' certificates. I hadn't forgotten about sciatica either, that king of simulated diseases. True, sciatica later proved useful to few people,

---

[1] Communist Youth League.

[2] Communist Party of the Soviet Union (Bolshevik). Members of the Communist Party and the Komsomol were the first to be executed by the invading German army.

for in the summer of 1941 tens of thousands of men, trying to save themselves from mobilization, simultaneously contracted this illness, so that finally, when someone mentioned sciatica, he was immediately branded a malingerer.

However, despite all my certificates, I was summoned one day for military registration. Two weeks later I was ordered before a medical commission, x-rayed, pronounced to have no diseases at all and found to be fit to serve. However, I still managed to retain my military card bearing the inscription 'exempt from military service', by declaring firmly that on a certain date I had surrendered it at the enlistment office to such and such a lieutenant.

Meanwhile, friend after friend received their call-up papers. At first, they went obediently, but growing numbers began to ponder how to avoid being conscripted. Obviously, I belonged to this group too, for it seemed to me not only cowardly and inane, but also ignominious to actively defend a government which had executed my father, exterminated our family, and failed to destroy me thanks only to a lucky combination of circumstances.

By the time I had received my first call-up notice ordering me to 'appear with cup and spoon', I thought I had found a way out: the institute where I was enrolled as a correspondence student was being evacuated to Central Asia. Firstly, I immediately registered as a full-time student. Secondly, using my 'clean card', I obtained a document stating that I was travelling with the institute. Thirdly, on the basis of this document, I had my name struck from the residents roll and the enlistment register at the city militia.

Then, placing a full bottle of vodka in my empty suitcase and ensuring that the neighbours saw me leave, I made as if for the railway station. Of course, I never reached the station, for on the way I dropped in to see my friend Oleg. A few hours later, leaving the suitcase and the now empty bottle at Oleg's, I slunk back through backyards to my lodgings, careful not to be seen. Back at home I had nothing to fear: the owners were 'have-beens' and as it turned out so was the other boarder – a communist and a member of the city council. Besides, the owners' son was at the front somewhere and they considered having me would be the best guarantee that someone would take in their son Volodka and care for him.

These were days when I felt victorious. As a consequence of my first seemingly brilliant victory in this war, I was able to dedicate my leisure time to such important matters as the purging of the Party. But that day, no sooner had I liquidated the letters 'CPSU(B)' than I heard a firm military step on the footpath outside. The person stopped, and I froze stock-still in anticipation. He banged on the door – my heart hammered in unison.

Had somebody informed on me? Or perhaps it was a call-up notice... But there could be no more notices for me. That could only mean... and here were these cards...

I stuffed them into a book.

Meanwhile I heard the landlady go to the door. The stranger uttered my name. Would the landlady have the courage to inform him that I had left, knowing perfectly well that I was in the apartment and unable to leave without being seen by the unknown visitor?

The conversation ended. The door slammed shut. The landlady returned. Alone.

Seeing me, she grew pale. Only now did she become frightened. Just as well it hadn't been earlier.

"Oh, my God! You're here. And I said you'd left. Hurry to your hiding-place – it was a call-up notice for you."

Behind the firewood, in the 'mouse nest' which for the past few days had served as my lodgings, I could sit cross-legged quite comfortably or even lie on my side, all hunched up. When my feet grew numb after such repose, I lay on my back and stretched first one leg, then the other into an opening above my head. Quite understandably, I would never have agreed to such a thing, but the landlady's tears and the landlord's fear condemned me to imprisonment in this, the smallest of cells I have yet occupied. On the fifth day I could stand it no longer.

I have an idiotic habit which I cannot be rid of: if I have business to attend to, I first complete work I have promised to do for others and then attend to my own. That's what happened this time. Returning to the apartment, I began on the military cards of my neighbour and his friend, although there were still personal matters that required my attention. Since my feigned departure had not helped me to evade the attention of the enlistment office, I had to visit Oleg, who worked in an establishment of military importance and thus was not subject to service in the armed forces, to see if I could get work there as well.

This time I brought my delicate work to a successful conclusion and took the completed job to my neighbour's room. The neighbour, together with his three-year-old daughter, was checking his library. The girl sat on the floor studiously leafing through heavy tomes, seeking out familiar portraits of Soviet leaders.

"With Uncle Lenin," she announced, "into the stove.

"With Uncle Marx, into the stove…"

A trusted Party man, the neighbour had to stay behind if the Germans appeared, to organize partisan resistance. Several barrels of honey and alcohol had already been cached in the forest, but there were no weapons yet, and it was doubtful that any would come. The neighbour was faced with a difficult dilemma: how to wriggle out of joining the partisans while keeping the honey and alcohol for himself.

Generally, the news was bad.

Call-up notices arrived for everyone, even those who had genuinely gone eastward, and those who had long since enlisted.

Even worse things happened: search parties with dogs appeared unexpectedly from backyards and snooped through basements and attics.

Next the authorities drew up lists of where they had searched and who had been taken in, and suddenly, as if continuing directly from our conversation, there came the sound of authoritative determined banging. The door opened, though we hadn't heard the landlady's steps. The corridor reverberated to the stamping of boots. We just managed to spread some newspapers over the documents which would have proved fatal for several people. I stepped out into the corridor. They were already knocking on the door of my room. 'Well, this is it,' I thought. 'I'll be lucky if I'm sent to the front line.' Spotting me, they turned around. Two militiamen.

"Does (they announced the name I used then) live here?"

I shook my head:

"Nah, he's no longer here. It's been a week since he left for Tashkent."

"Hm… Tashkent… Who can testify to this?"

"I can, if you like."

They handed me the notice. Usually, Soviet establishments muddled up the letters of my invented surname, but this time it was written correctly. We entered the room – papers and drafting instruments remaining after the purging operation were strewn across the table.

I sat down and wrote obliquely across the notice in green ink: 'So and so (name and surname) departed for Tashkent on September 27, 1941.' I signed with a nice but indecipherable scrawl.

"Thank you, comrade. So long."

They took the notice and left. At the door they bumped into the landlady carrying buckets; she'd been to the hand-pump for water and had forgotten to lock the door.

"And who's this, your mother?" one of the militiamen asked amicably.

I gave an affirmative nod of the head: yes, my mother! The landlady looked up in surprise: how could it be that they had come for me, saw me, and yet left me alone?

Desperate insolence is absolutely the best counter to any danger, so my good humour improved immediately, and I even began to cherish the hope that I had put the militia off my trail for good, and that they would never return. However, the landlady was of a different opinion. She was seized with fear after I told her about my conversation with the militiamen, which was quite perverse on my part. She was convinced the militia had already deciphered my signature and would return any minute.

'Maybe I should go to Oleg's?' I thought. 'He's not troubled by notices, and I could hide at his place.'

Slipping through backyards, I came out onto the street. My boots and a gas mask slung across my shoulder gave me a semi-military appearance. Men whom I occasionally passed in the street, glanced at me in fright. I even felt like approaching some of them and demanding their documents. But instead of Oleg, I was met at the door by his scraggy older sister.

"Oleg? He was called up a week ago."

The news stunned me. Oleg, who had 'protection', Oleg who loved to recite Yesenin's autobiographical poem 'Anna Snegina', applying it to himself:

> But I did not take up the sword;
> To the rumble and roar of mortars
> A different courage I displayed:
> I became the first deserter.

Could this Oleg really be in the army? No, he was probably just in hiding and they did not want to tell me.

Once again, my spirits fell. I even forgot to ask about the suitcase and books which I had lent Oleg. What could I do? Look for Oleg in his hiding-place? Return to the apartment? In any case, I couldn't remain in the street. I returned, anticipating another horrible stretch in the 'mouse nest'.

But I never hid in the wood-shed again. I reached my apartment as it was growing dark. Already there was a light in the window. I peeped in just in case, for these were times when one could expect anything, and froze for a second. A soldier was sitting in the room. Swiftly and silently I recoiled from the window, but returned after a few minutes. And then I noticed that the landlady had a happy, tear-stained face, and there was a bottle on the table. The photo of her son Volodka, which hung on the wall, and the stranger sitting beneath it looked strikingly similar...

Volodka had to begin his story from the start for me.

He had been in a unit which was encircled at the front, and after the unit had been routed, he had made for home. The stories which he told were fantastic, but it was precisely this which made them alluring.

Leningrad was surrounded, the front was supposedly now near Moscow, although in reality there was no front, only separate ragtag units in retreat. Weapons were few, usually one rifle to several men. Rations consisted of a glass of millet meal every two days; nobody cared whether you ate it raw or cooked. For two months they did not change their underwear. The Germans took no prisoners – everyone was sent home. Ukraine was ruled by a hetman[3], a Gogolian Taras Bulba. In German-occupied territory

---

[3] An elected Cossack leader from the 16th century and later.

they had opened churches and liquidated collective farms.

I believed his words, because I wanted them to be true. After all, the truth behind any statement depends on two factors: the authority of the person making the statement and our desire that it be true.

Doubt starts to creep in only where either of these components – desire or authority – is missing.

The evening passed in lively conversation, but as the hour of sleep drew near, a question suddenly arose: which of us would go into the hiding-place – Volodka or I? Both of us were deserters and it was equally risky for either of us to sleep in the apartment. However, the 'mouse nest' in the wood-shed could accommodate only one person. There was neither time nor space to make another hiding-place.

I faced one further complication. The enlistment office continued to harass me with call-up notices, sending militiamen to fetch me. Were they to come and discover both Volodka and me, it would appear to the owners that I was responsible for the loss of their son.

Now my presence was not only superfluous, but also undesirable. So, leaving the hiding-place to Volodka, I slept the night in the loft and left the next morning, ready to accept whatever the future might hold.

EXECUTION

1

While I was still inside the carriage, I learned that the train would be going no further. But then I never had any intentions of going further. I had set out with a definite plan: to reach the city of N., find my countryman, and stay with him until the front had passed. Leaving the station behind, I realised I had arrived too late: home guardsmen were everywhere, armed with gas masks and bottles of inflammable liquid, the streets were riddled with trenches and barricaded, and there was hardly anyone outside. This meant the front was nearby and it was dangerous to walk the streets. Home guardsmen, militiamen, and the occasional Red Army unit were the only people in the streets. I was eyed with suspicion, but left alone.

Bad beginnings end badly: my countryman no longer lived in his old apartment. Luckily though, I was given his new address. I scribbled it down gratefully and began wandering among the anti-tank trenches, knife rests and barricades. On one corner I took out my pad to check whether I was on the right track, and immediately realised that I was making the biggest mistake of my life. In wartime who else but a spy or saboteur read or wrote something in the street while in civilian dress? Before I could find the page with my friend's address an obnoxious character materialised before me.

"Citizen, your documents please!"

My documents were faultless — a permanent passport and a 'clean card' exempting me from military service.

Despite this I heard the fellow order me to follow him so he could 'establish my identity'. He took me to the militia station, and from there two militiamen escorted me at gunpoint to the enlistment office where my documents were taken and I was turned over to a soldier on his way to the home guard staff. At the staff post I was registered, fed, and sent in the company of a home guardsman with a hunting rifle to 'take up a position' at some half-dug ditch in the middle of a street which I had to defend. It became apparent that I was already a home guardsman of the Nth company, whose objective was to stop the advance of Guderian's[4] twice-routed tank formation with the aid of bottles filled with an unknown liquid, and shotguns...

Don't think that I let myself be led about obediently and submissively followed their orders. I argued and protested... Especially when trying to prove the needlessness and irrationality of the order to have my hair cut by the staff barber. In the end I imagined I was dealing with automatons, each programmed to carry out only a single function, and who, because of their mechanical nature, were incapable of doing anything other than what their master had assigned them to do.

At first, I thought that at the slightest opportunity I would desert my fatuous post and continue the search for my countryman. Three days passed and the opportunity to escape presented itself at every step, but I remained. Not because I was afraid of the patrols and spies who controlled the streets and could detain me, and not because I feared the round-up conducted each night in one part or another of the city. I was simply interested in turning a new page, so unlike all the others, in the book of my life. As always, I was much too sure of myself, certain that at the last minute I would be able to avoid confronting the enemy on the battlefield, would manage to reach my countryman and sit out the danger there. However, I wasn't too overjoyed at having no papers — even my 'military card' remained at the enlistment office.

Every day brought with it something interesting and unexpected. We would be put on point-duty and forgotten for ten hours or more, standing in the icy autumn rain soaked 'through to the bone and even deeper', as the saying goes. Or they would bring the latest military invention, a 'Partisan' grenade, and teach us to use it: take out a box of matches, light the grenade fuse and then throw it onto an enemy tank. Heavy, clumsy ancient rifles were issued one to a section.

No-one was interested in the grenades. Some of the fellows tried firing the rifles, though this was forbidden. It turned out that most of the rifles were inoperable — something was wrong with the bolt. But no one cared. Apart from a few sixteen-year-olds no one really

---

[4] Heinz Wilhelm Guderian was a German general during World War 2.

intended to fight the Germans. It was another thing to fire a shot or two into the air on point-duty. Among both young and old the greatest interest was generated by the bottles of inflammable liquid. What would happen if you drank it? The older men recalled the tsarist times when people were still so backward that they drank neither methylated spirits nor varnish. They didn't know, you see, thought you couldn't drink it, but when they tried it: 'Ah, so that's what it's all about!' And the men sighed, remembering the magical taste of methylated spirits.

The men in our section bore little resemblance to those in a regular army unit. People who could have been turned into soldiers had long been conscripted into the army proper. The home guard consisted of minors, old men, semi-invalids, and at best unsuccessful deserters and malingerers like me. The oldest were in their fifties, the youngest fifteen or sixteen. The adults believed that the youngsters needed to be watched so that in the event of any trouble they would not begin firing at the Germans. Among the adults I knew of only one man, an unshaven fellow with a Chapayev[5] *papakha* hat perched atop his head, who was not ready to greet the enemy as saviours. I don't know what we were supposed to do according to him, but he expressed his dissatisfaction at every order and action of our immediate command. When we were issued with the latest grenades which exploded with the help of a match, he mumbled:

"Russia is going to rack and ruin, and they're playing with dolls!"

2

Reinforcements stopped arriving on the third day. In compliance with some order, everyone suspected of being a deserter was to be immediately shot instead of being assigned to the home guard.

I was returning drowsily from guard duty, where I had spent from seven till eleven that night. Beside me walked a soldier from a neighbouring company. He was telling me how they had executed

---

[5] Vasily Chapayev was a celebrated Russian soldier and eccentric Red Army commander during the Russian Civil War

a deserter that evening. "A silly young lad. His father died, so he wanted to bury him. Left the unit at night and sat by his father's side for two whole days. Made the coffin himself, there was no one else to ask. Well, they came for him. He wanted to hide, scrambled up into the loft. But they dragged him down and brought him before the commander. The *politruk* [6] ordered him to be shot. We'd just returned from duty detail, so the *politruk* picked me and our squad leader. 'Take him to the cemetery,' he said, 'and shoot him.' We took him there. He was white as a corpse, teeth chattering. 'Boys,' he said, 'I want to lie beside my father. I dug a grave for him over there yesterday. Shoot me over my father's grave.' We began to search but couldn't find the grave. It was a dark night, the rain was pissing down, matches wouldn't burn. It's an enormous cemetery. He led us round in circles, but there was no grave. Our squad leader, Mitka Khardikov, you know him, everyone here does, asked: 'Going to annoy us much longer?' We really thought the lad might be trying to escape. You know yourself, the cemetery's full of bushes and trees, it's a veritable forest. When we first started getting to know girls, it was where we would take them. Too many people in the city park... So we'd go to the cemetery. Well, we thought: the boy's decided to escape. The rain began to pelt down, and he said: 'My father's grave has to be somewhere here. I know it is, I just can't find it.' We walked on a bit, the path took a bend. Our wet clothes were sticking to our skin. And Mitka Khardikov bellowed: 'You bastard! How long are you going to toy with us?' He rested the rifle against his shoulder and — bang! The fellow threw his arms out, reeled, and stretched out across the path. Dead. Mitka pumped another one into him point-blank. We stepped over him, took some twenty steps, and then saw the pile of black earth and a freshly-dug hole. We felt a pang of regret at not having brought him to his father's grave."

No sooner had I dozed off, when the command to fall in rang out. We were assembled in the staff passage. The atmosphere was tense. The home guardsmen were afraid they would be forced to retreat. No one wanted to retreat, for nearly all were resident in the city. A factory was in flames nearby and heavy oily smoke spread

---

[6] *Politruk*, short for *politicheskii rukovoditel'* (political instructor).

across the street. The night paled in the fire's flames, darkness scattered and melted away. In the passage we could just make each other out. There was no electricity, for the power station had been dynamited so it wouldn't fall into enemy hands.

A small group of men emerged from a room. In front was a man in a long coat; behind him the lieutenant tensely held a rifle at his neck. Next came the *politruk* and several staff personnel. They stopped before our ranks. A command sounded: we were to be issued our orders. One of the commanders lit a lamp, and in its light the brightness of a hand holding a sheet of paper became engraved in the darkness of the passage. Immediately the greyness of dawn in the windows became a thick solid wall.

Accentuating every word, a voice began to read the order:

"In the name of... is to be shot... for desertion..."

The person in the long coat was to be shot for desertion. A vivid picture appeared in my mind, as if I had seen it myself, the vision of a fresh, still empty grave and a body not twenty yards away.

And then, quite unexpectedly for those who thought they had come to know me these past few days, I stepped forward and announced:

"Comrade commander! Allow me to execute this man."

"Surname?"

I replied.

"Which section?" I named the section. "Good lad!"

The commander turned to the home guardsmen to see who else would volunteer to shoot the convicted man.

A fifteen-year-old youth, one of those who had really wanted to fight the Germans, stepped out.

The commander looked him up and down.

"Can you shoot?"

"Yes."

"Used an army rifle before?"

It turned out that the lad had never fired a proper military rifle before and had only used a shotgun. He was ordered back into line.

The question rang out once more, needling the hearts of the men: "Any other volunteers?"

But there were no more volunteers, and it became apparent that someone would have to be assigned to the job.

20

The light of the lamp slid up and down the rows. Standing in front of the line near the group of commanders, I realised that the thought which had entered my head would occur to no-one else. Nearly every one of these civilians was unused to weapons and to most of them to execute or to be executed was equally terrifying.

The light of the lamp rested on a face. I knew this man, for we belonged to the same section. He was a cobbler, aged forty-nine, and people sneered that he whispered prayers at night.

The cobbler was ordered to fall out. They asked him if he knew how to shoot.

Yes, he could, he had fought in the civil war. But he had just come off duty and was tired.

"That's all right, you can rest later."

They asked the cobbler his surname, then took us aside and announced our immediate assignment: to take the person entrusted to us to the cemetery and shoot him. I was put in charge of the operation.

"Understand your assignment?"

"Yes, comrade commander!"

We were issued with rifles. The lieutenant who was standing motionless behind the person in the long coat surrendered his place to me. But my companion, the cobbler, protested. He wanted to walk behind the condemned man, I had to walk in front. Though he gave no grounds for his demand, I realised that he was afraid of leading the way. So, holding my rifle at the ready I stepped in front of the condemned man. The cobbler fell in behind him. Now we could go. We moved off.

We left the staff post, turned a corner and were enveloped in a silence broken only by the crackle of a nearby fire. Fires were burning everywhere. I counted eight. And that was only beyond the river in the part of town I could see without turning my head. The sky was cloaked in clouds which reflected the dancing red flames and seemed to move, to change their form, but this was probably only an illusion. Where there were no fires, the sky seemed almost pitch black. When the flames died down, the clouds above seemed thicker, lower, and when the flames reared up the clouds grew brighter, appearing limpid and feather-light.

It was a little frightening. What if the cobbler mistook some uneven step of the condemned man for an attempt at escape and fired in fright?

I discounted the possibility of an actual escape attempt. People, as far as I know them, fear disobedience above everything. The fear of punishment for disobedience is greater than the fear of death. True, I was being followed by a deserter who had already tried to resist. But it is one thing to clamber into a loft without seeing immediate danger, having read a call-up notice, and quite another to run away from two armed guards. However, it is at these moments that heroes are born. Thousands of people have escaped from the firing squad at the last minute. How could I be sure this one wouldn't bolt? I didn't know the reason for my certainty, but I walked freely, completely relaxed.

And when the white gates of the nearby town cemetery loomed before us, the cemetery to which we were sent only because of its proximity, I experienced a fleeting shadow of the feeling which others in my place had probably felt too: the pleasure of domination. I had absolute power over a man, power over his life and death. The awareness that I was only a tool in my enemy's hands had dissolved. I could shoot the person walking behind me here or there, a few minutes earlier or later — and this was enough to create the illusion of free will.

That is why those who go into battle to die for other people's truths, following orders from above, feel they are heroes and do not realise that their heroism is only a transposition of their fear of punishment for being disobedient.

As for me, I have always been disgusted by the heroism of a slave who dies for his master. In the case of a slave killing for his master, I had ideas about that too. But now wasn't the time for reflection.

We approached the cemetery. The twilight became soupier under the old leafless chestnuts.

A light autumn shower sifted through the sieve of clouds and pricked my face and hands with thin icy needles.

The cobbler was breathing heavily. We had hurried and he was tired.

I knew the cemetery a little. I had passed through it this morning, actually yesterday morning, for it was now one o'clock.

To the left, in the farthest corner of the cemetery, past the bare bushes of lilac, cherry, hawthorn and briar, past the old chestnuts and elms, was the place where I had seen the fresh graves. There, twenty paces from an empty black hole, lay a corpse. I intended taking the person in the long coat there.

*   *   *

I ordered a halt and stopped. Then turned to the two behind me.

"Here?" the cobbler asked me.

"No, not here, I know where..."

I approached the cobbler.

"Listen, Uncle Vasia..." (Maybe he was called something quite different, it didn't worry me). "If you don't want to take part in this business, I'll take care of it myself. Wait here. And when you hear my shot, fire into the air or wherever you like, as if we fired together."

The cobbler's sullen expression seemed to brighten. But he hesitated. It would be a breach of discipline, a failure to obey orders.

I gave him no time for reflection and took up his position almost forcefully. A few short commands and we proceeded. The two of us. The cobbler followed us for several steps and stopped.

We turned off the main path and continued along a track lost among the bushes. White crosses emerged from the darkness. The trees receded. In the distance, beyond the ravine and fields, a village was burning. Perhaps it contained military targets and now they were being destroyed?

Something black lay across the path... Everything was a monotonous grey on such nights: the clouds, the earth covered with fallen leaves, the wet trees. Only a person could stand out black against such greyness. Yes, we had reached the spot. The executed man lay on the path.

It all looked different to what I had imagined in the passage, as I heard the execution order. There were no bushes here, the grave was not visible, the dead man lay in a different pose.

Three steps remained to the body.

I raised my rifle and aiming over the head of the fellow before me, fired into the night, into the emptiness, into the distant glow playing on the clouds. And immediately a shot echoed from the chestnuts. How tensely the cobbler must have been expecting my shot to be able to fire only one second after me!

What did the fellow in the long coat feel now? How could I tell? He stopped uncertainly, for there was no order to halt, and turned to face me.

"Com… comrade…" his lips tried to articulate. But I slung my rifle over my shoulder and ignored his words.

"Well, that's it," I said. "I've executed you. That's you lying there on the path. Do you understand?"

"No… no, I don't."

"Darned fool. I was entrusted with the execution of a man whom I brought here and shot. There he is, lying on the path at your feet. And I haven't a clue who you are."

The man in the long coat remained silent. Trying unsuccessfully to comprehend.

I grabbed him by the sleeve.

"Get the hell out of here before I smash your face in!"

This helped. The man seemed to wake up, tried to ask me something. I could detect no special joy in his words. Hadn't he believed me yet?

Does the fear of death consume a person so completely, that even after salvation it continues to possess them, stopping joy from entering their heart? Or does the expectation of death rob us of so much strength, that after evading destruction we are unable to express joy straight away? I don't know the whys and wherefores, I only know that joy never comes immediately after intense suffering.

But I had no time for reflection and conversation.

"Get!"

Turning around, I walked away.

Someone was coming toward me. A stranger? No, it was the cobbler. Even so, what did he want? Come to check on me?

"That you?" he called out.

"Yes, it's me."

"Well, how'd it go?"

"All done."

"Who were you talking to?"

"Me? Talking? You must have been dreaming. Although… maybe after all this business I really did begin talking to myself."

Somehow, I had stopped in my tracks and the cobbler was approaching me slowly, still nervous, his rifle drawn. He came level with me.

"Let's go and take a look…"

"What the hell for?"

"Maybe he's still alive?"

"Even if he is, he'll be dead by dawn."

The cobbler pressed on, I followed him. The body lying across the path became visible. The cobbler hurried up to it. If he was so interested, let him take a look.

The cobbler came up to the body and uttered a scream.

"What's the matter?" I asked.

"It's not him," the cobbler said in fright. "It's not him! The fellow was wearing a black coat, this one's dressed in a pea-jacket."

"He was probably hot and took his coat off," I said angrily. "Come on, let's go!"

"It's not him," the cobbler repeated. "What have you done? You've let him go free. What will happen now? Oh my God! We'll be shot tomorrow just like this fellow for failure to carry out orders."

"God Almighty! Really, Uncle Vasia," I said. "We were charged with the execution of a man. Which is what we did. That's him lying on the path there. No one will come to check, and if someone does, they'll find an executed man and be satisfied that we carried out orders. Forget about the long coat. Besides, you must know… in the far corner of the cemetery, near the demolished church, lives the caretaker, the same one who digs up fresh graves, undresses the bodies and sells the clothes at the flea market. At least that's what most caretakers of our cemeteries do. So, it wouldn't be at all amiss for him to remove the coat from the executed man and leave him lying in a vest or jacket."

25

At this moment somewhere nearby, a cannon blast thundered as if from the other side of the gully behind the cemetery. A whistle in the air was followed by a hollow explosion in the city centre and the chatter of machine-guns, sounding like rain on a tin roof.

Had I known that the Germans were so close, that the battle was to begin so soon, I could have desisted from arranging this mock execution, and not fooled the cobbler and tortured the condemned fellow. Now it was ridiculous to return to our unit.

I placed a hand on my partner's shoulder:

"No one will ask us tomorrow whether we carried out orders. Tomorrow there will be a new master in the city. Meanwhile, throw away your rifle and go hide somewhere."

OUR SIDE HAS ARRIVED

1

There are no statistics yet about the number of times I've had to flee and hide in my lifetime. But I don't think I've ever had to flee or hide in such an unpleasant situation, under such unfavourable circumstances.

To escape during the day, one only needs to dive into a crowd and become lost in it, jump onto a moving tram and then hop off unnoticed, or best of all enter a courtyard and emerge into another street. It is easier to escape at night, under cover of darkness. But now there was a war. And because of the curfew the streets were empty, apart from the occasional home guardsman on duty and the stray 'combat battalion' of NKVD[7] agents.

I was unfamiliar with the city, having spent only two or three months here several years earlier. In that time, I had become acquainted only with the area I was living in and the city centre, as well as the streets in my friend's suburb. Besides it was spring then. Now it was autumn, yards were filled with bare fruit trees, leafless bushes of raspberry, gooseberry and redcurrant. The buildings looked wary and mute. The last uncaptured deserters trembled in dark corners. No one would let a stranger into his house. My countryman, Petro Oplenia, lived on the other side of town. To reach him I would have to pass the home guard staff headquarters near Borshchahivsky Bridge. All the other bridges had been blown up.

Everything was against me.

The gunfire subsided. Maybe the Germans were already in the city? Or perhaps it was only the Soviet Army clashing with its own reinforcements, a frequent occurrence. They say that during the Polish incursion the Orel Division was annihilated in one such clash. An eyewitness had told me: 'They brought only the flags back to Orel'...

---

[7] The precursor to the KGB, the Soviet secret police. The initials stand for *Narodnyi Komissariat Vnutrennikh Del*.

I peered into windows, tried to open closed gates and locked shed doors, struggled through wire fences and scaled walls, unable to find a suitable place to shelter. People are never so cowardly as after a heroic act. Then they allow themselves the luxury of fear.

Finally, I found a yard which seemed safer than all the others.

But hardly had I made myself comfortable under cover on some firewood, when the street filled with the sound of steps and muffled voices. A detachment of soldiers was passing. When the stamping began to recede, curiosity got the better of me. I slunk up to the gate and peered out. Immediately recoiling, I clung fast to the fence post. I couldn't be mistaken at such close range. The *politruk* and the commander of our home guard unit had just walked past the gate. The home guardsmen were being moved to the outskirts of the city. The Germans must have been somewhere close.

At this moment shots rang out again and I was buoyed with courage.

Should I try?

I gripped my rifle. I would step out into the street, kneel on one knee and, without hurrying, aim first at the commissar and then, if I was lucky, at the *politruk*. The distance between them and the home guardsmen was enough to guarantee me a safe escape.

I peered out carefully. Looking ahead I saw two dark figures slowly receding. Further on, at an intersection, the last ranks of guardsmen were rounding the corner.

I looked back – a human figure was making its way up the street toward me.

Foiled again...

But this tension needed a release, and when only a few steps separated me from the fellow, I blocked his path and, raising my rifle, ordered in a muffled voice, almost whispering:

"Stop!"

The person stopped and began calmly:

"I'm one of ours! Private, second company. I know the password. Take me to the commander of the guard..."

The word 'guard' seemed to stick in the soldier's throat. He changed all of a sudden, as if frightened of something and froze, raising his hands.

28

"Into the yard!" I ordered in a whisper.

The man obediently entered the dark opening of the gate. I looked in the direction the commissar and *politruk* had gone, but there was nobody to be seen. They had probably turned the corner too.

In the yard the trees and buildings were engulfed in darkness. I spotted the rifle behind the soldier's back.

"Lie down!" I ordered him and he lay down compliantly.

I recovered the rifle from his shoulders.

"You can get up now!"

The home guardsman rose to his feet.

I really didn't know what to do with him next. He knew probably no more than me about the plans of his own command or that of the enemy.

"You're alive?" he suddenly addressed me.

"Sure. Where do you know me from?"

"We're from the same unit... In the home guard... You and Komariakin took the deserter away today to be shot."

I grimaced. Someone had remembered me and, as luck would have it, I'd probably be turned over to the Germans tomorrow or the day after as an NKVD agent who executed deserters. A foolish story!

"Well, and what happened?" I asked offhandedly.

"Well and... Komariakin returned, said that you had escaped and let the deserter go free."

"Returned?!"

"He was immediately executed for failure to carry out orders. They looked for you but you weren't anywhere to be found. Later the *politruk* read out an order that you and Komariakin were sentenced to be shot and that 'the order had been carried out'. We thought you'd been caught somewhere and finished off on the spot."

I laughed.

Then I learned that he was returning from regimental staff where he'd taken a report that the Germans were already in the nearest village, that they were firing on the bridge, and that the home guardsmen had marched to the front lines to confront the enemy – probably to the gully on the outskirts of town.

I released the soldier, keeping his rifle. Then I felt ill at ease again. What if he didn't heed my advice to return home, and instead came back with a detachment of soldiers? True, I had had a cigarette with him and we seemed to part friends, but who knows...

It would be safer to move somewhere else. And the rifles? I would take one with me and throw the other one away. But which one was mine? I studied both carefully, but they were identical and in no way differed from one another. I checked the cartridges – each had three in the magazine and one in the barrel. I unloaded one of the rifles and took out the cartridges. With the rifle now empty, I leaned it against the fence in the darkest corner.

The horizon was turning grey. Soon it would be dawn. Where could I find shelter?

Around me were strange empty streets, locked, ominous buildings, the fallen leaves of bare orchards, wooden fences and barbed wire.

Then I saw a small house with its door wide open and windows smashed in. The occupants were probably communists or 'responsible people' who had been evacuated earlier.

Have you ever had to enter the black emptiness of a strange house at night, rifle drawn? If only you knew what a luxurious feeling it is!

It became light.

The room where I had dozed for about an hour was completely empty, apart from a smashed cupboard. A large window, with no glass or frame, looked out onto the orchard. In the adjoining room stood a heavy closet. A rusty bed lay on its side, and a magnificent volume of a jubilee edition of Pushkin's works lay open on the floor.

I knelt over the book wanting to pick it up, but pulled my hand away as if it had touched a burning-hot coal. The book was stuck to excrement.

2

There was no battle, really. The Germans did not appear from where they were being expected. The soldiers sat on the far side of the gully, open to fire from the rear. On this side of the gully they were vigilantly guarded by the commissar brandishing his Mauser and the *politruk* with his semi-automatic. So the home guardsmen sat quietly and stayed put, leaving their 'custodians' with nothing more to do.

Mortars sailed overhead and landed somewhere far away. Machine-gun rounds filled the whole suburb with clatter. Observant people would have noticed that the gunfire was not coming from the immediate vicinity, but actually from some distance away.

The silent buildings seemed empty.

I have yet to meet a person who was completely devoid of fear. There are people though on whom fear of a certain type has no effect. A person who puffs on a pipe and looks indifferently at falling bombs may not dare approach the edge of a precipice. A tightrope walker who calmly traverses chasms, may have a morbid fear of spiders or frogs, and a general who is afraid of neither bombs, nor sheer drops, nor spiders – may be scared of his own wife.

I had no fear of the machine-guns or the tanks, in other words everything which had caused the city's inhabitants to close their shutters and hide in their cellars. I was only afraid of the commissar and the *politruk* whom I was out to get.

But I still continued to move in their direction.

I had almost reached the spot where they were sitting, peering from time to time around the corner to see if the Germans were coming or the home guardsmen retreating. But all was quiet. Even the mortar attack had ceased.

I could see them through a crack in the gate. From here I could hit my mark easily, but the gate was locked and the fence was higher than me. I needed to change my position. I set off between the houses. Suddenly I was forced to turn around.

Dressed in a white wedding dress with a dirty train and a garland of everlasting daisies on her head, a strange woman flitted like a butterfly from the door of the nearest house.

"Isaiah, rejoice!" she sang from the doorstep. "Our men are coming! Our men are coming!"

"A madwoman!" I thought.

And maybe because I thought this about her, she suddenly focused all of her attention on me.

"And who are you, a fugitive? Well escape, escape! Only you must throw away your rifle." At these words her eyes met mine. "Or maybe you want to shoot some cute commissar? Well, that's different then."

I winced. My innermost thoughts, sealed so impenetrably all these years from my friends and enemies, were an open book to this madwoman.

"You'll do right, young man. Because an armed deserter ceases to be a deserter – he becomes an insurgent, a new dialectic category. As Comrade Marx once said, a class in itself becomes a class for itself."

She roared with laughter, spun her train around and ran off singing, "Isaiah, rejoice!"

I was awestruck and returned to my earlier position to look through the same crack in the gate.

Suddenly the woman in the wedding dress appeared in the street. She ran with a skip and headed straight for the commissar and the *politruk*.

"Isaiah, rejoice!" she sang into their faces. "Our men are coming, master officers!"

The commissar said something to her which I did not catch.

She broke up in laughter:

"Not yours, comrade commander, ours." And she sang again: "Isaiah, rejoice! This virgin has conceived and will bear a son and his name will be... Adolf!!!"

Her strong resounding voice could be clearly heard above the rumble of the distant gunfire.

The *politruk* said something to the commissar, the commissar said something to the *politruk*.

A thought flashed through my mind: 'They're going to shoot her!'

I pushed the rifle barrel under the iron latch on which a lock hung, and ripped the latch off with a soft crack, which was lost in the gurgle of machine-gun fire. As I opened the gate, I saw the *politruk* raising his semi-automatic at the madwoman. She was laughing with her reverberating voice:

"Perhaps you want a flower to remember me by?" she asked, and took the garland from her head.

The commissar and *politruk* stood facing her, with their backs to me.

"*Hände hoch!*" I shouted, pointing my rifle at them.

They swung around together and their faces turned the colour of the madwoman's dress. They recognised me, the soldier whom they had executed in absentia. The *politruk*'s revolver fell to the ground. His hands rose awkwardly.

"Isaiah, rejoice! Our men have come!" the madwoman yelled joyfully as she ran past me.

Neither the commissar, nor the *politruk*, nor I, stopped to think why she was yelling or what she saw.

I moved closer. Thirty, even twenty metres seemed to me far too great a distance to aim well.

Who would be first?

The commissar, of course!

I aimed at his chest and pressed the trigger. The lock clicked dryly – there was no report. I threw out the dud shell and slid another into the chamber. Again the same result. The rifle would not fire. Obviously, this wasn't my rifle, but that of the soldier whom I had disarmed.

The commissar's eyes crossed mine, he twitched violently, jumped back and drew his revolver from its holster.

But he neither managed to shoot me, nor I to hit him.

Something buzzed and whistled nearby, then exploded close behind me. The commissar jumped like a hare and bounded over the fence; the *politruk* rolled over heavily after him. The madwoman yelled out in pain. Only then did I turn around. Near the gate from which I had emerged, the madwoman was thrashing about, trying to get up.

A block away soldiers in green were marching down the footpath. A tank crawled slowly down the middle of the street. Uniformed soldiers sat atop it like bizarre black horsemen.

Germans!

They had come from the town, from the rear, from where nobody had expected them.

And instead of saving my own skin, I ran up to the wounded woman. Bullets whizzed over my head again, but I managed to drag her in through the gate. The Germans were still far away and before they arrived, I would be able to disappear.

Why had they fired at her? She had been across the street from us...

The woman opened her eyes and looked at me – there was no madness in her eyes – and she said with bitter irony: "And I thought they were on our side..."

And then I remembered that not three hundred metres away, in positions exposed from the rear, sat soldiers and their commanders. Armed with grenades which did not explode, with bottles of liquid which did not ignite, and occasionally with rifles which did not fire. They had not yet realised that their guardsmen had disappeared and that German tanks were approaching them from the rear.

But there was no time to warn them.

PRISONER

1

What's that book in the corner, next to the red one? That thin
one. Ah, it's Vynnychenko's 'Mockery'. An interesting book. Very
interesting. Though you know, I don't agree with it. I can't imagine
a situation, such as Vynnychenko[8] describes, in real life. The book
is supposed to demonstrate the primacy of matter over mind and
attempts to persuade the reader that physical torture, even ordinary
pain, are more intense than mental suffering. For materialists who
have denied their spirit, it is probably so, but for those of us who
have even the poorest of souls and have no wish to disown it, there
exist certain spheres which the body, with its joy and pain, dares
not penetrate. I too found myself in the position of Vynnychenko's
hero. The circumstances were quite different of course, but the
nature of the incident was the same. It was in the spring of 1941.

Everything happened as I had expected. The completed and
unfinished trenches failed to hold back the German tanks. A
detachment of home guardsmen armed with bottles were encircled
and machine-gunned down. A 'combat battalion' of several dozen
NKVD men dispersed without a shot being fired, and a Red Army
platoon which was probably in the city by accident, crossed the
half-frozen river after sporadic fighting and disappeared into the
nearest forest.

There and then I decided it was high time that I had a decent
meal, a good sleep, a shave, a wash, and made myself look
respectably human. (I must add that I hadn't had anything to eat for
a day, no sleep for two days, and hadn't shaved all week.) All this
would become reality only after I found my countryman, Petro
Oplenia, whose address I had in my notebook.

I was walking along a deserted street in his neighbourhood. It
was quiet, much too quiet. Suddenly an elderly man shot out from
around the corner at a youthful sprint and disappeared through a
gate or door into one of the houses. It happened so fast, that I didn't

---

[8] Volodymyr Vynnychenko (1880-1951), an eminent Ukrainian writer and
statesman.

even notice which one. Even before I realised that the danger from which the stranger was fleeing could threaten me too, I was already at the nearest gate trying hard to open it. The gate was high, securely locked, and unyielding. I could probably have forced the gate, or scaled it, I even might have made it to the fence or found some other way to disappear, but I regained the ability to think soberly and decided that my attempt at escape was a cowardly act. The best thing would be to reach the corner and satisfy myself that there was nothing there to flee from. However, it is often most unwise to trust one's own judgement.

I reached the corner and recognised the neighbourhood: it was the same corner where several days earlier I had been stopped by a plainclothes militiaman. It was a fateful corner!

"*Iwan, komm!*" a voice rang out, more like the bark of a metal dog than a human voice.

I looked around.

Several German soldiers were leaving a nearby house. What did they want from me? Acting very flattered by their attention, I came up to the group.

"Vas vollen zee, bitte?" I addressed them, thinking they would ask me directions.

Without uttering a word, a tall soldier with a square jaw punched me in the face. This had not been the first punch I had received in my lifetime. I had hit others, others had let swing at me, but never had I received a punch which affected my morale so much. I had, in the past, been beaten deservedly and for no reason at all, by people armed and unarmed, both after receiving warnings and unexpectedly, and even with odds of twenty-five to one against me. Some had aimed to insult me, others to kill. In other words, I was accustomed to blows. However, until now I had been faced with militiamen, drunken carters, city hooligans and bandits. But these were soldiers of the best army in the world, in whom I expected to see representatives of a real culture, untainted by Bolshevism, the bearers of the spiritual uniqueness of Wagner, Goethe, and Kant, the children of a country which had produced unrivalled examples of music, poetry and philosophy.

I was baffled. I did not know what to do – whether to run away or to stay and fight the Germans… Indeed, for some minutes I lost my ability to think.

"Watch!" the German shouted.

Full of preconceived ideas about Germans formed mostly from books, I did not understand what was required of me. I thought I was being asked what time it was. And even after the soldier tore off my wrist-watch and pocketed it, I did not immediately grasp what had happened. And for a long time afterwards I comprehended nothing, passively accepting all that occurred and postponing its evaluation to a hazy future. My knowledge of people did not extend to Germans, and my ability to anticipate events vanished with the arrival of the new masters of my life and my death.

The Germans moved from house to house and rounded up all male inhabitants from fourteen to seventy. In several minutes the street was teeming with lost and slightly frightened old men and teenagers.

"Three!" a soldier shouted, raising three fingers into the air.

We fell in three to a row, forming a long column, and when there were enough of us, we slowly moved off. Fresh streams of people joined us from neighbouring streets. People emerged voluntarily from homes missed by the Germans and hesitantly joined the column.

I looked around to see if my countryman was in the crowd, but he was nowhere to be seen. I asked the fellow beside me why we were being herded together and where they were taking us. He eyed me inquisitively up and down and said nothing. I turned with the same question to my other neighbour, who was one of those who knew everything. He explained that we would be registered. "They're going to check our papers and stamp our passports."

'I wonder,' I thought, 'where they'll put the stamp on mine, seeing's as I haven't a passport?'

We were passing a large unfenced garden when some distance away an officer caught sight of a person carrying a sack among the trees. The person probably wouldn't have heard the usual shout of 'Iwan, komm'. The officer pulled out his pistol, took careful aim and fired. The person with the sack stopped, turned his head in our

37

direction, then continued on his way. The tall soldier, the same one who had detained me on the corner, went down on one knee and raised his rifle. Just then we turned a corner and I only heard the crack of the rifle. I never learned the fate of that person with the sack.

"Know where they're taking us?" someone said. "To prison."

And really, the column was already nearing the prison. The word *"Halt!"* rang out. We were kept in front of the prison for several hours, but weren't taken inside. At nightfall they herded us further through the deserted muddy streets.

It was quite dark by the time we reached an enormous yard which our black throng, numbering several thousand, filled to overflowing. I pushed my way inside a three-storey brick building and found a room less crowded than the others. Here I slept until the morning on an overturned wardrobe.

The red glow of cigarettes glimmered in the corners of the pitch-black room and the broken window etched a formless stain on the wall. My neighbours were talking about the Germans and the events of the day. They were convinced that the round-up of all men to one place was an easily explicable and lawful action which the German command found necessary. They anticipated the arrival of German goods and believed that free trade would begin soon, together with a freer life.

I made myself more comfortable and dozed off. As I drifted off, I became aware of a dull ache in my mouth.

2

The first thing I realised when I awoke in the morning was that I had toothache. My teeth had never bothered me before and I even wondered on occasions what a toothache would be like. But I had been spared the experience then. The pain came now, uninvited and unwelcome, at a time when there was no dentist, no medicine, not even ordinary aspirin.

The pain grew worse, intensifying rapidly, killing every thought, engrossing my whole being, blocking out the world and becoming the centre of my existence. Because of the pain I accepted everything happening around me as something secondary, even disregarded it. But I should not have been indifferent. Our passports were not being stamped and no one was registering us or asking for our documents. We were simply counted and declared prisoners of war. True, there was the occasional military greatcoat among us. The Germans weren't at all interested in registering our names or establishing our identities. With our scant knowledge of Germans, we thought the whole incident was just a ploy on the part of the local Command, who were boosting the number of prisoners to make their victory seem greater than it really was.

In the meantime, the city was overrun by soldiers. Who was there to stop the looting and violence when most of the male inhabitants were behind barbed wire? There were, however as my companion Vania, a Red Army soldier, told me, relatively few cases of rape. A man had been shot for trying to protect his fifteen-year-old daughter, and a woman had been forcibly separated from her husband and was found bayonetted to death in the morning. But these were isolated incidents. Instead, the Germans looted, seeming to move systematically from house to house.

The fact that we were not given food bothered me. True, most of the prisoners were locals and their wives and mothers brought them food, so they were not haunted by the prospect of death by starvation. But apart from the locals, the camp contained some two hundred Red Army soldiers (who knows where had they appeared from, for during the 'battle' for the city there had not been a soldier in sight…), several dozen Poles from Western Ukraine, who were conspicuous by their clothes and manner of speech, some communists from the district centre, and the random deserter.

I had hardly had a bite to eat the two days before my capture, yet the toothache was stronger than my hunger and it prevented me from feeling anything, even from thinking.

After three days in the camp, I was beginning to feel like the *Untermensch* or subhuman painted by Germany's racial theorists. I had exchanged my new coat for an old quilted army jacket and two loaves of bread. The bread had been stolen right away, and a German guard had ripped the jacket with his bayonet. A slender corporal had relieved me of my boots, ordering another prisoner to give me his galoshes. My cheeks were covered in stubble and had become so hollow that when I was finally able to wash on the third day, my hands did not recognise my face.

Vania approached me once and asked: "Sink your teeth into anything today?"

"No, nothing."

"Here," he said, breaking off half a loaf of fresh bread. "Stuff that into you... They pass it on from home."

Vania was a sharp fellow. He knew that anything polite like 'Please, help yourself!' would be out of place here.

I took the bread and wolfed it down, using the left side of my mouth, for the right side was all ache. Thus, the problem of food was accidentally solved. Two problems remained: escape and the toothache. The solution to the first seemed to depend entirely on the second. 'As soon as the pain dies away, I'll escape, I'll think of something.'

But the pain continued unabated. In fact, it grew worse. During the day I tried to fight it, convincing myself that my teeth didn't really hurt, directing my thoughts to other things far removed from pain. But the nights were pain's paradise.

Three days passed. Two, three times a day we were lined up, counted and inspected. Boots, warm clothes, even good caps were confiscated.

Vania still came and brought me food. Why? What on earth for? What good turn had I done him? Because of the pain I hadn't even thanked him properly. A German officer appeared with an interpreter in a deerskin coat. He ordered us to hand over all gold, knives, and watches. Anyone disobeying the order would be shot. In addition, we were told that for every German killed, ten prisoners would be executed. The officer refused to answer any questions. After he left, twenty prisoners were picked from among us, lined up against the walls of a demolished power station and shot. The scene was visible from the windows in the left wing of our building. I did not look and so the event probably scarcely touched my consciousness, having no profound effect on me, neither upsetting, nor shocking me. The question of my own or someone else's death did not interest me. Let them kill, let them shoot! What upset me most was that the aspirin which Vania gave me had no effect.

Nothing else mattered, neither what was happening around me, nor my own predicament. Everything depended on my aching tooth and nothing else. Ordinary toothache wouldn't have been so bad. That kind of pain would have been restful in comparison to this. But alas, it came very seldom! Normally the sensations of pulling, twitching, jerking and twisting alternated with a kind of combined pain which included all these and was impossible to name.

3

The morning of the fourth day was the most dismal autumn morning I can remember. A huge grey cloud hung motionless like a heavy concrete ceiling, whose weight pressed down on our shoulders. The fog either thickened, accompanied by a cold drizzle, or it lifted a little to expose the ghostly forms of wet roofs, dirty walls and bare trees.

As usual we were lined up in threes, but the routine command bore an undertone of something special. Today everything was different. No one was ordered to take his boots off. All the old men were called out and ordered to step aside. Two or three dozen German soldiers were waiting for us at the gate and on the ground near them was a pile of shovels, spades, and picks. A red-headed sergeant counted off one hundred and fifty of us, including me, and ordered us to grab the shovels.

"*Schnell! Schnell!*" the soldiers yelled, prodding with bayonets those who were slow to obey. Here we were in a column once more, with shovels on our shoulders. We were marched out into the street. The sergeant counted us again — there were only 149. A fellow was walking down the street with buckets: the retreating Bolsheviks had blown up the water-main and the populace had to walk two kilometres to fetch water.

"*Komm!*" the sergeant shouted at him. The man stopped. A soldier raced up to him, tore the buckets from his hands and using his bayonet forced him to join the column. We set out.

Though I was walking with my eyes glued to the ground, perceiving nothing except my pain, I intuitively sensed that the attention of the whole column was directed at one point. I raised

41

my eyes. Near the steps of a stone building ten men lay on the wet leaf-covered earth.

'Where are they taking us?' I thought. 'Maybe they'll line us up against some wall and...'

We were approaching the outskirts of the city. More and more we passed empty lots overgrown with dry thistles, large orchards, unfenced vegetable plots, and only here and there the occasional cluster of small, three-windowed suburban dwellings.

"May I inquire as to the purpose of our little walk?" I asked the guard in classical broken German. The guard gave me a sullen look and said:

"Quiet!"

We were walking between the Jewish cemetery and the endless brick wall of a former artillery depot. Ahead of us a dog was running alongside the wall.

Suddenly the sharp, dry crack of a rifle sounded from the middle of the column. Knowing that Russian soldiers could never resist the temptation to shoot at stray dogs, I looked in its direction. But the dog continued calmly on its way.

And then the realisation that we were surrounded by Germans, not Russians, drove home that something frightening and irrevocable had occurred.

"*Schnell! Schnell!*" I heard in my ear.

Those in front were jogging past something on the road, trying to stay in threes.

"*Schnell! Schnell!*"

Even before I learned the truth, I knew something dreadful had happened. I felt the exhalation of death upon me as people feel the breath of an enemy come to kill them.

A few more steps...

On the road, flat on his back, eyes turned back into their sockets, red froth on his lips and one hand pressed to his chest lay a boy wheezing with a heavy death rattle.

"Why did they shoot him?" I turned to my neighbour on the right, hardly able to move my tongue, which had become unwieldy and disobedient.

"Quiet!" answered my companion in a muffled whisper.

42

Everything: the endless brick wall, the Jewish cemetery, the gloomy guards with drawn rifles, the spades on our shoulders and yesterday's visit from the tall officer, the ten dead in front of the building, and now this poor boy senselessly killed — all merged into one terrifying unity. Suddenly everything was clear: we were being taken outside the city to be shot. We would be forced to dig a mass grave and would then be shot.

An animal captured and caged throws itself violently at the iron bars of its cage and chews until it can break free or collapses exhausted. People in similar circumstances remain outwardly calm, but their thoughts pounce madly in all directions like caged beasts.

Firmly pressing the shovel to my shoulder, I marched in silence like the others, but my thoughts rushed ahead of me, tripped up, fell down, and rose again. And then, among other things, I noticed that my toothache had vanished without trace, engulfed by the fear of death. My whole being was filled with the premonition of an immediate, senseless and dishonourable death, leaving no room for toothache.

What should I do when commanded to dig a ditch? And afterwards, when they lined us up along the edge?

Should I drop to my knees before the officer and beg him to spare my life, lie to him that I was born a German, that I would join their army voluntarily? I would be shot before uttering the first sentence!

Or should I raise the shovel over my head and with shouts of 'Kill the bastards!' split the skull of the nearest German, grab his rifle and... But how do you fire a German rifle?

Would anyone listen to me? Would they obey my order and attack the Germans? Perhaps only one or two would respond, and the rest would stand motionless, like a flock of sheep, looking on. I estimated there were 150 of us and 25 to 30 of them. Even if only every fifth man heeded my call, if every fifth man in our column was a hero, we would secure our freedom and our lives. But even if such an act brought death from bullet or bayonet, it would be an honourable, noble death, with nothing to fear or be ashamed of.

I prepared myself, tense, as if awaiting a command. 'Oh, if only someone else would give the order to attack! If only someone else would take the initiative!'

How easy it is to submit to another person's will! Yet how difficult it is to lead others and make them obey!

Unbidden memories suddenly surfaced, overshadowing reality. Memories of loved ones. Never does a person experience such a closeness to the people near and dear to them as in the so-called 'borderline situation', when they are on the brink of death.

...The face of a lost friend, my only true friend. He was no acquaintance or casual companion, but a friend who had risked his own neck to save mine. A girl's face. Short cropped hair, not a beautiful figure, but such unforgettable golden eyes. I didn't even say goodbye to her when I left, for neither of us suspected that we were in love.

And then from the dimness of the distant past, the tears of sorrow in my mother's eyes when father and I were arrested. And father's muted words of farewell when I was moved from the death cell because I was a minor: 'If you ever get the chance – escape!'

There were no guards nearby, so I touched the shoulder of the fellow in front of me:

"Listen, when you hear my order to attack, chop down the nearest German with your shovel and run!"

There was no answer.

Instead, the fellow on my right said quietly:

"You're crazy!"

What else could I do?

I did not become a leader. And I'll never make a leader, because the only person I'd be able to lead would be myself.

We left the cemetery far behind and finally reached the end of the brick wall of the former military depot. We were coming out into open countryside.

And then somewhere in the darkest corner of my mind there stirred a timorous thought: perhaps we would not be shot after all, perhaps we were just being led off to work.

Who said we had to be shot in a cemetery? Couldn't they shoot us by the roadside? The column came to an intersection and we heard the command to stop. An officer and several guards huddled together to discuss something. Obviously, the end was near...

An incomprehensible command rang out. Our column shuffled off slowly along the old highway.

With every step hope grew stronger and stronger, eventually bursting into the certainty that no one was going to shoot us, that we were being led toward the front lines to do some work, perhaps to clear land mines or build a new bridge in place of one that was destroyed, but most probably to fill anti-tank trenches.

When we were stopped before a dug-up section of road two hours later and told to level it, the spectre of death left us. They might still shoot someone for an offence or for no reason at all, but not everyone would be executed. And then slowly, uncertainly, like a detachment returning to its abandoned position, my toothache returned.

Then I remembered the book I was now holding. Perhaps, I thought, there was a certain mockery in the realisation that physical suffering even at its worst takes second place to the suffering of the spirit, but that is not the mockery Volodymyr Vynnychenko had in mind.

After a while I again lost the ability to feel and think, and again it appeared that the only thing which mattered in the world was my aching tooth. There was no war, no armed Germans, no slain comrade, not even the fear of death – none of this existed.

A FRIEND

1

This was one of the Soviet Union's strategic roads. It was wide and straight, and like the famous Vladimirka[9], it too ran due east. Recently cows and sheep, Red Army soldiers and home guardsmen were herded along it. Here the genius of Soviet military art was revealed. The road was designed only for the movement of their own Soviet armies on foot: motorised enemy formations could not move along it, for it had neither asphalt nor even a gravel surface.

Our task was to repair this road in order to make it passable to German transport. For the third day in succession we remained in the hands of the ordinary Wehrmacht, rather than one of those special units whose responsibility it was to guard prisoners of war, and whom the people took for Finns, unable otherwise to explain their unwarranted cruelty.

We were housed at the edge of a village in several houses strung along this strategic road. In the house in which I found myself, the menfolk had been evacuated by the retreating Soviets, the wife and children had moved in with relatives, and an old granny had stayed behind to guard the house. Her presence created an air of domestic warmth. No one seemed to be guarding us and indeed there was no real need for a guard. We were all so tired and exhausted that none of us even thought of escape. Besides, the general consensus was that 'we had been arrested by mistake and would be released any day now'. True, I have never relied much on general consensus, remembering that 'truth never rests with everyone, almost never with the majority, very rarely with the minority, a little more often with single people, but most often with no one'. However, I was so exhausted by several days of toothache that I intended to rest a while and did not hasten to devise any escape plans.

That first evening a red-haired sergeant-major, speaking in the most incomprehensible German dialect so that I couldn't understand a thing, gabbled angrily about something to us.

---

[9] A road along which prisoners were taken on foot to Siberia before the building of the Trans-Siberian Railway.

"Versteht ihr?"

"Nane," someone answered.

The German hit the fellow over the shoulders and swore. Then he spoke again, more fiercely and incomprehensibly than before. This time when he asked if everyone understood, I answered with my head bowed, so he couldn't tell who was replying:

"Yavol, main herr!"

The German swore again and left.

We brought in some straw and began making ourselves comfortable for the night.

The company I found myself in consisted for the most part of city riff-raff or *shpana*, as they were known. These were not the true *urkas*[10] who knew the passwords and rules of underworld ethics, but hooligans with several convictions, whose dearth of criminal experience gave them immunity against the fear of mobilisation and helped them hide out until the arrival of the Germans. They knew one another and formed a tightly-knit circle. Outside this clique remained a lost Jewish boy; a Vologda youth from the trade school, who stood out because of his enunciation of the letter 'o'[11]; two or three nondescript types, and myself.

The next evening, while I was getting ready for bed, one of the hooligans made himself comfortable on my straw.

Somehow I managed to win back my place without a fight, but the next day, when we were being served lunch, several men yelled out:

"He's already eaten!" and someone else received my portion of food. Such an incident was an ill omen.

And then it occurred to me that perhaps in one of the houses nearby there was an heroic individual, a person of strong will and great sincerity who could help, sustain and rescue me. It seemed a meeting with this person would immediately solve all my problems.

---

[10] The *urka* belonged to the middle classes of the Soviet criminal underworld. The highest class was the hardened criminal – the *blatny*.

[11] As opposed to mainstream Russian, where the 'o' is often pronounced as an 'a'.

In the times of Alexandre Dumas the sign of a resolute, daring, energetic, noble person, in other words a hero, was an aquiline nose. Later, apparently as the result of the light hand of Jack London, the sign became a hard-set chin. True, the character of a heroic person had changed somewhat. Thoughtless temerity was replaced by tenacious dedication. However, this was only a variation on the same type of person.

Some of the Germans who escorted us to repair the road had hard-set square jaws. But this did not symbolize heroism. The frightened Jewish boy, who was in the same group as me, had an aquiline nose, but he did not symbolize heroism either.

My hero had a 'potato' nose, a soft almost feminine oval face and was called Vania.

Usually, the most radical approach to solving a complex problem is to escape. So the best thing now would not be to dream of a hero, but simply, out of habit, to flee. However, not knowing the surrounding countryside, I couldn't escape alone, and I couldn't seek a friend to escape with from among the hostile *shpana*. My ignorance of the hinterland produced a serious obstacle to escape primarily because of the proximity, twenty kilometres or less, of the 'front', that is, a village where the remains of Soviet military formations were stationed. At night I could easily lose my bearings and stumble onto them and this prospect was not at all appealing.

A temporary solution appeared in the form of a cheerful young soldier from Vienna. This Viennese soldier hit no-one, did not abuse anyone, forced no-one to work, and didn't even walk about holding a stick. He whistled Strauss instead, and eagerly talked with those who knew a little German. His duty was to oversee our group of prisoners, but he left us to our own devices and strolled about everywhere, saying: 'Karasho[12], karasho!'. Following my request, the Viennese let me join his group in the end house adjacent to the fields.

Although the new surroundings in which I found myself did not, at first appearance, especially appeal to me. In the middle of the house I had entered someone was being beaten up, or about to be. Two fellows had each other by the shoulders. Actually, one of

---

[12] Pidgin Russian, meaning 'good'.

them, who had a red face with wide cheek bones, was holding another who was trying to break free. A black-haired man was trying to hit the restrained fellow in the face from behind someone else's back, but was afraid to move closer and could not reach him.

A tall sturdy man a head taller than me had raised a log and was hesitating whether to clobber the restrained fellow or not.

"Kolia, let him have it!"

"Flatten him!"

"Over the noggin!"

The crowd egged on the assailants.

The youth at whom the crowd was directing their fury was Vania, the Vania who had brought me bread and just the person I had wanted to meet.

"Land him one with the log, Kolia, the log!"

The red-faced fellow tugged at Vania's shoulders, the tall fellow pushed someone out of the way so that he wouldn't miss, and readied the log in his right hand...

"Wait, I'll do him in myself!"

All heads turned in my direction. Who was I and why should I become involved?

"Here, I'll finish him off!" I repeated, approaching Vania.

The crowd parted. All eyes were riveted on me. The arm of the tall man remained poised. Everyone in the room froze in expectation.

I came up calm, authoritative, confident.

"Who do you think you're wagging your tail at?" I asked Vania, stopping between him and the red-faced man, separating them. I hit out, but stopped my fist short of Vania's face... Swiftly I swung back and elbowed the red-faced fellow in the nose, I think, and then, turning sharply, landed a right under his jaw...

This is a tried and tested 'method'. Make out as if you're attacking your own man to disconcert the enemy.

Now the tall man could easily reach me with the log, but like everyone else in the room, he had been initially taken aback, and a moment later Vania had him by the shoulders and was pulling him down onto himself, jumping up at the same time and striking the fellow in the face with his head.

49

Once, twice, three times…

The third time Vania pushed hard and the tall man's skull hit the wall with a hollow thud.

"Hi!" I said, offering Vania my hand and only now noticing that he was no longer wearing his Red Army uniform and was in civilian dress.

He shook my hand and, turning to the red-faced man who was picking himself up off the floor, to the tall fellow wiping away blood, and to all in the room, said:

"Any questions?"

But there were no questions. Only a loud comment sounded from the back of the room:

"I told you this chap would show them."

2

In general, the men here were the same as in the first group. The same *shpana*. The same obscure grey figures. Only in place of the Jewish boy and the fellow from Vologda there was a queer tenth grade mathematics teacher and a scraggy character in a leather jacket. This character reminded me of someone. I even asked Vania:

"Who is he? He reminds me of someone."

"He reminds you of a Bolshevik from the Civil War," Vania replied.

How true. The leather jacket, the diagonal blue breeches, the boots concealed by rags tied around them, the face with a chekist's[13] wrinkles around the mouth — everything evoked a transplanted decorative Bolshevik. But I thought that he most probably wasn't a Bolshevik, because it wouldn't have entered a real Bolshevik's head to dress so theatrically. Hadn't I seen other Soviet prisoners in leather jackets? Hadn't I myself gone about in officer's boots and with a gas-mask to conceal my identity? And his face was far too sickly, yellow, emaciated. The face of a broken man.

---

[13] Belonging to the Cheka, the first of a succession of Soviet secret-police organizations, established in 1917.

I forgot about him.

The following evening we were lying side by side on the dirty straw which covered the damp earthen floor in a thin layer and philosophised. Actually, it wasn't Vania and I philosophising, but our neighbour, a mathematics teacher, a greying man who for some unknown reason was placed with the young men during the sorting.

"Now, man is nothing more than the tiniest mathematical quantity, a two-billionth part of the whole called mankind. Individuality, as such, no longer exists. We are living in the age of functional automatism. Nothing depends on the individual any more. People are led off to fight, and they fight. They are taken prisoner, and they die from hunger and cold. They die and nobody is responsible for their deaths, just as you are not responsible for the people you kill in war. You automatically execute only a certain function, completely divorced from your will. If for some reason you are incapable of performing this function, you will be replaced by another person, like a broken cog in a machine. The only consolation is that someone will one day place flowers on the grave of the unknown soldier..."

As much as I like philosophy, I can't stand philosophising, all the more since he spoke as if he were teaching in class and we, his students, had to sit at our desks and listen reverently.

I interjected:

"Excuse me. What has the unknown soldier to do with this? After all, we're the Unknown Deserters! This is something far greater than your unknown soldier..."

"Don't sneer at things which are sacred to all of mankind." The teacher grew indignant. "No one has yet built memorials to fallen deserters nor brought flowers to their grave."

"Because deserters are immortal!" Vania said.

The teacher wanted to reply, but Vania, who was eavesdropping on our neighbours, commanded: "Shush!"

There really was something worth listening to. A youth, who had already spent time in a large transit camp, was recounting his experiences:

"We were herded into a large pit. There were ten, maybe fifteen thousand of us. The Germans stood guard with machine-guns. Anyone who poked his head out was shot. No food, no water. There was a river nearby, they could easily have fetched us some water, but no — *verflucht* and *verflucht*[14]. Then one day we saw a horse grazing at the edge of the pit. We had Uzbeks among us. They tied a lasso from some belts, one of them crawled up to the top and threw the lasso onto the horse's neck. And then yanked with all his might. Everyone pitched in and pulled. The horse put up a fight. But finally, it fell straight on top of us. We were like animals. Would you believe it, we tore the live horse apart with our hands. And ate it raw."

"You were proposing some theory about the immortality of deserters?" the teacher asked, returning to our conversation. "You want to stay neutral in this war which has embroiled the entire world?"

Vania lifted himself up on his elbows:

"So what, if the whole world is at war? It doesn't concern me, because I'm not fighting. And he," Vania pointed at me, "isn't fighting either. And if everyone performed their moral duty, just as we are doing, there would be no wars."

But a mathematical mind can't be swayed by youthful ardour.

"War, my dear fellow, is a historical regularity which occurs, as has been proven a long time ago, not only despite our petty desires, but also despite the will of those who rule us: presidents, kings, and dictators. And you with your rebellious personality can do absolutely nothing for others or even yourselves..."

"Have you read Kuprin[15]?"

"I have."

"Do you remember his story 'A Dog's Happiness'?"

"Can't say that I do."

"It's about a smart dog. A stray dog caught together with others by dog-catchers and brought to a tannery where dogs are skinned alive, so the pelt is softer. And while the other dogs submissively awaited their fate, which they no longer had control over, this miscreant showed them in whose hands a dog's happiness lay – it jumped the fence and fled. So there's nothing particular to argue

---

[14] Damn! (German)

[15] Aleksandr Kuprin (1870-1938) was a Russian writer best known for his novels *The Duel* and *The Pit*.

about. Tomorrow he (a reference to me) and I will be escaping and so disclaiming your philosophy by way of our actions and not just through words. The snow has frozen over a bit — in the event of anything happening, we could lay low in a ditch, and we will be able to travel cross-country, without our feet sinking too deeply in the snow. If you want to join us, you're welcome, but if you're afraid, stay behind. Later, when we're behind barbed wire, it will be more difficult to escape."

"Actually, I think this is some kind of misunderstanding and we'll be set free any day now. I'm not a soldier. And I've got all my documents – my passport, military card, union card..."

"Well, that's your business, but we... we'll show you in whose hands a dog's happiness lies."

At these words the door opened and the red-haired sergeant-major entered. Mitka, the clumsy interpreter, slipped in after him. The German gabbled away rapidly and at great length.

The interpreter reduced it all to several sentences.

"We have learned that some of you plan to escape. But remember, there are thirty of you here and you must watch one another. For if even one of you escape, the rest will be shot."

And they left.

I remembered that on the first evening this same German had come and obviously given the same speech. But then he had been without an interpreter and we were unable to understand a thing.

Although the danger of being executed was now added to the constant danger of being killed, the teacher sounded victorious:

"Now you must be convinced that we are only a minute part of some whole, and not at all individual quantities. One escapes, the rest are executed. Here your individuality is not taken into consideration, your personal freedom means nothing. You will be executed not because you are good or bad, not because you have committed a certain act which is punishable, but only because a certain number of prisoners must be executed. Maybe there are sadists and wretches among those who execute, but the system will not change if they are replaced by honest, morally pure people. Everything is reduced to mathematical calculation."

"Now there are thirty of us," I interceded. "If one escapes, the rest will be executed. In other words, $30 - 1 = 0$. In my opinion, mathematics has nothing to do with it. This is plain idiocy, nonsense, stupidity."

3

Vania and I were filling in an anti-tank trench and were seeking a solution to the current situation. The problem before us was indeed formidable. If we escaped, the others would be shot, of that we were certain. If anyone else escaped – we would be shot.

"What's worse: to commit an offence or to become its victim?"

"If we stay behind, and assuming no one else escapes, we'll still die, if not of hunger, then of cold. In several days, after we have repaired the road, they'll obviously put us to work on the bridge. That spells death. Or they'll lock us up in a camp... So, we need to escape. But..." I deliberated aloud, conferring with myself and Vania.

"There is a way out!" Vania interrupted me. "Everyone needs to escape!"

"And the guard?"

"We can eliminate him!"

I shook my head in disagreement.

"Then you don't acknowledge," Vania attacked me, "our own theory that each individual bears full responsibility for taking part in collective crime. Our Viennese guard had a free choice – to become a deserter like us, or to go to war and kill us. He chose the latter. So we have the absolute right to kill him. If you deny this, it means you're in agreement with that fool," Vania pointed at the teacher. I shook my head again.

"You see... the fact of the matter is... This Viennese, whom you so casually suggest we kill, is the only humane German of all the ones we have had cause to meet. And to eliminate him would be quite unfair. Besides, ten of our men will be shot to avenge him. And since neither you nor I will make up that ten, it means ten innocent people will be killed because of him."

"Well what alternative is there?"

"Distraction. You and I can keep the German talking while the others escape. Over there behind the logs lies an abandoned Maxim machine-gun. You and I will take the German over to show him

54

the Maxim, and meanwhile all the boys can escape. When we see they've disappeared, we'll twist his arms, gag him, and clear out."

Just between us, of all the plans I have ever carried out or tried to carry out, this was undeniably one of the stupidest. For the German might realise that he was being distracted, might notice the escape, and could possibly turn out to be stronger than the two of us. But Vania belonged to that group of people who first try to realise a scheme, regardless of whether it's their own or someone else's and, only in the event of failure, begin to look for reasons why the approach failed. So the first person to voice doubts about my plan was not Vania, as should have been expected, but I myself:

"What if everyone doesn't want to go? Our mathematician, for instance. Try to convince him to escape!"

"The mathematician will be the first to come. We will tell him that according to the calculations of some Clausewitz[16], a certain percentage of prisoners must inevitably escape. And he'll come along. 'Automatically'."

"Fellas!" Vania said to the boys. "He and I," he pointed to me, "will keep the German occupied while you escape. Because when they shove us into a camp behind barbed wire, we're done for. You'll get out of there."

Silence is rarely a sign of agreement. More often it is a protest people are afraid to voice. However, we knew the mood of the prisoners: the certainty that we would be released was starting to waver, a fear of the future appeared together with a desire to return home. We also knew that the prisoners were not so much afraid of the treatment they would get at the hands of the Germans, nor of the hunger and the cold, as they were of the breakthrough of Soviet divisions westward and that our camp might be captured. Those who had been in the Red Army faced execution for failing to observe a paragraph in their oath containing the words: 'Soldiers of the Red Army do not surrender or allow themselves to be taken prisoner'. Meanwhile, those who had not been in the army would be shot under article 58-1a of the RSFSR criminal code. And it was

---

[16] Carl von Clausewitz (1780-1831), a Prussian general and military theorist who stressed the "moral" and political aspects of waging war.

55

only twelve kilometres to the nearest village where some Soviet divisions were stationed, we were reliably told.

For my part I addressed the prisoners in almost the same words as Vania.

I don't know whether it was because the others viewed our escape plan as unrealistic, or simply that people perceive the good you try to do them with the utmost hostility, but the replies we heard were:

"Escape yourselves if you're so keen!"

"We're not that stupid!"

... Well? The escape would probably need to be postponed for several days, and in the meantime each man would have to be persuaded separately.

On bleak November days dusk arrives early. The merry soldier from Vienna was whistling the 'Blue Danube' and counting us before releasing us for the night. Suddenly his whistling stopped, his face changed, becoming wary, foreign, impenetrable. Other parties of prisoners moved past us, on their way back from work. The Viennese called out.

Several soldiers marched up to us. We, who had become unaccustomed to any form of discipline with the Viennese and had kept in a disorderly mob, were being regimented in rows and our column was counted twice – from head to tail, and from tail to head.

There were twenty-nine men instead of thirty.

Someone had escaped.

That familiar sensation of death lurking nearby was awakened. It stirred and moved, rising and filling me with spine-chilling coldness.

But in opposition to it there arose from the depths of the soul, where no thought enters, an affirmative and categorical: 'It can't be!'.

People who have had to await execution, and then managed to evade it, are convinced that their experience is universal and that everyone else in similar circumstances will feel, think, and act in the same way as they did. However, as in love, each time there is something different about the fear of death...

The guards talked among themselves and calmed down.

At last we were driven into the houses as usual and given dinner...

As it turned out, none of the *shpana* placed much importance on someone's escape, for no one believed in the likelihood of collective responsibility – that we could be shot for someone else's transgression. The guilty person stayed free, nobody looked for him, no one hunted him, and the innocent were shot for his actions. This seemed completely ridiculous and was beyond comprehension.

When I reproached those who had foiled our plan of mass escape by hinting at the possibility of execution, I was told:

"Quit stirring up panic!"

Our mathematician, as befits a person who forms his own opinion about everything, but one that was always contrary to the actual state of affairs, said to us:

"You'll be to blame if we're shot."

"Right. Who else? Only I can't see why."

"Because you incited us to escape. So the fellow escaped."

"Maybe he escaped earlier?"

"He went into the willows to do his thing in the morning and never returned," said one of the more obscure characters, joining our conversation.

"You know him?"

"Sure. He's one of ours, from Briansk. You must've noticed him too, always went about in a leather coat."

"Leather coat? Simonov!" I exclaimed.

"Yeah, Simonov," replied the man. "Why, are you from Briansk too? How come you know him?"

"He was the governor of the N-sky Detention Centre," I told Vania. "I'll tell you about him one day. I should have recognised him straight away."

'I should have recognised him straight away...' I repeated to myself and became absorbed in reminiscences.

I must have begun to doze off, for I was suddenly awakened by a breath of coldness. Not the coldness from the door which had just been opened, but from the words of the man who had just entered:

"There's a guard outside. They won't let anyone out."

And as if to substantiate his claim, a terse '*Halt!*' echoed outside like the retort of a rifle.

Vania did his shoelaces up again, having begun to untie them. I adjusted the string with which I had tied the galoshes to my feet.

My consciousness, which had just categorically ruled out the possibility of execution, was probably in reality not my own consciousness, but a reflection of the general consensus, accepted and confirmed as my own.

Did the psychology of my surroundings have the power to influence me too?

"Make a break for it?" Vania said with a shade of inquiry in his voice.

"Make a break for it!" I said. "Through the window, maybe?" We came up to the window in the back wall of our house. But it was too late.

German soldiers burst into the house: our Viennese, the red-headed sergeant-major, and some other private. They had brought two unshaven, middle-aged characters in home-made village garb with them.

"Who speaks German?" the private asked.

Vania stepped forward:

"I do."

Both fellows immediately mobbed him, gibbering away in Russian and pleading with him, pushing pieces of paper into his hands:

"Comrade translator..."

"Translate for him!"

"We're deserters..."

"Here's our pass. We're on our way home. It says here we can go home and no one will stop us."

"*Diese Mensche sind Fluchtlingen,*" Vania translated. "Sie wollen nach Haus gehen. Sie haben ein Durchlassschein."

"Was? Durchlassschein? Wo ist Durchlassschein?"

Vania took the 'pass' from the hands of one of the fellows. Looking over Vania's shoulder I tried to read what was written there in Russian.

Pass this around!

Comrade Red Army soldiers, officers of the Red Army!

The Jewish communist government headed by Dzhugashvili-Stalin has violated its treaty with Germany.

THINGS HAVE COME TO WAR!

Through the near-sighted politics of your friends you have been forced to spill your blood for the THIRD INTERNATIONAL.

... When the venal tsarist regime was toppled, the communists promised you land and freedom. BUT HOW THEY HAVE TRICKED YOU!

... What good is such a government!

... Down with Stalin and the communists! Freedom for all workers!

This was no pass.

"The other side, the other side," one of the fellows prompted. Vania turned the leaflet over. The other side bore the words:

Pass.

The bearer of this pass having no desire for thoughtless bloodshed has voluntarily left the Red Army and is crossing over to German side assured a warm reception awaits him. This pass is valid to cross territory under the German control to place of residence.

The thing that struck me first was the illiteracy of the 'pass': the absence of commas and the incorrect structure of the last sentence. Obviously written by a German, I thought.

Vania began to translate the contents of the pass. The two fellows looked on with satisfaction. But when Vania reached the words '*Die Rote Armee*', the German stopped him:

"*Was? Was?*" And turning straight to the men, asked: "*Seid ihr russische Soldaten?*[17]"

"*Soldat! Soldat!*" agreed the deserters, poking at their chests, glad that they were understood.

The German would not listen to any more. Hurriedly he exhaled several sentences, from which I gathered only that these characters were prisoners-of-war and would remain here in our camp.

---

[17] Are you Russian soldiers? (German)

Vania translated this. The deserters' faces became drawn again and they hammered away together:

"But the pass..."

"Home, it says here, 'to place of residence'..."

"Where you two from?" Vania asked.

"Minsk, in Belarus. We're both from the same village."

Vania addressed the Germans again:

"But they both have passes..."

"*Das ist kein Durchlassschein,*" the German said angrily and added: "*Ein Stuck Toilettpapier ist das*[18]. A real pass must be written in German and is only valid with the stamp and signature of the area commander."

4

While we were removing the mud from the road, we noticed that our shovels struck something hard and rocky from time to time. We began to clear away the mud and from under half a metre of earth there appeared an old cobble-stone pavement from tsarist times. Under Soviet rule the road was not repaired and had gradually disappeared into the mud.

"This is probably the 'Trajanus Road' mentioned in *The Tale of Igor's Campaign,*" Vania exclaimed.

"After capturing Troy," I backed him up, "the Roman emperor Trajanus continued along this road all the way to Moscow."

"Trajanus? To Moscow? I don't seem to recall any such thing," the mathematician responded.

"Of course. Didn't you study Klyuchevsky[19]? Remember Tsar Ivan the Terrible, who was then stationed in Aleksandrova Sloboda, addressed his bodyguards with the now famous words: 'Dear comrades! Brothers and sisters! The savage Roman fascists have attacked our homeland. But the enemy will be annihilated, comrades, victory will be with us![20]'"

---

[18] That is no pass. It's a piece of toilet paper. (German)

[19] Vasily Klyuchevsky (1841-1911), a leading Russian imperial historian.

[20] A parody of Stalin's speech to the people of the USSR.

The teacher realised he was being ridiculed and moved away angrily.

The Belarusians, who were working with us that day, eyed us with hostility. Who knows, maybe they blamed Vania for their predicament.

We heard the other lads question them: 'How are things there?' as if it could have changed 'there' in such a short time. Fragments of sentences reached us:

"Nobody's changed their underwear since the start of the war. The lice are eating us alive. Haven't seen any bread for two months. Two or three rifles are issued per unit. Reinforcements arrive in civilian dress..."

The Viennese recognised the fellows and addressed them in a friendly voice. But they didn't understand. He came up to us:

"You are very lucky. You weren't shot yesterday only because there was no officer, and now that these two have appeared, you have one in reserve."

We looked at each other.

Hardly had the Viennese moved away, we began to argue.

"You escape!"

"No, you!"

"You know the countryside better."

"But you need to be rescued first. I'm stronger, I can survive longer."

"Yes, but you've got a mother, and I haven't got anyone."

"That's no reason."

I tied a knot in one corner of my handkerchief. Then I showed him two identical ends:

"The knot escapes. Pull one."

Vania pulled out the knot.

"Twenty-three Rosa Luxemburg Street, formerly Third City Street, Petro Matviyovych Oplenia," I said to him. "Don't forget."

Vania repeated the address. Then took the addresses of the mathematician and a few other fellows who had supported us during arguments, and shook my hand...

I've parted with close friends on many an occasion. Yet when *I* left, even knowing it would be forever, I always felt a rising tide of energy. On the other hand, seeing someone off, even for a short time, has always left me lost, sad, and depressed...

It was the same this time. All night after Vania's escape I was tormented by bad dreams. I woke from the cold: my feet were frozen. My galoshes must have fallen off during the night. I felt about with my hand – yes, the galoshes were gone. And they weren't anywhere nearby. I trembled at the terrifying suspicion that one of the *shpana* with whom our relations had been strained from the very start (though there had been no more fights), had taken into consideration that I was alone and removed my galoshes to pay me back for their recent defeat.

* * *

The roads were already dusted with snow, although it was not the first snowfall for the season. Snow had fallen for several days back in October. Harsh frosts could be expected any day now, and here I was barefoot! I would perish for sure...

Well, I had chosen my own fate. I could have escaped with Vania and thus sentenced the rest of the men to execution, just as the theatrical but real Bolshevik, Simonov, had done, but I had remained to share a common fate with the rest of the prisoners.

A day passed, and another. I never even suspected that I was so hardy. I got hold of a horsecloth, cut it up and sewed myself some unusual footwear. The remainder of the horsecloth I wrapped around my legs and strapped it down with string. Mine weren't the only feet to look like this. Most of the prisoners wrapped their feet in the most bizarre rags.

Our work on the road was finishing. The anti-tank trenches were filled, the mud which we were unable to shift, froze over during the night, paving a steadily better road for German transport. But several large puddles in the deep ravine had stubbornly persisted. We chopped willow branches with spades, carried them in bundles and built dams across the puddles. I was so intent on stepping on dry land where possible that I didn't at first realise that everyone's attention had been directed for some minutes at an unusual sight.

Along the road leading from the town to our camp several women were descending into the ravine. These weren't local

62

villagers. Peasant women were easily recognisable by their clothes and their ambling gait. There were eight or nine of them.

"Some mothers are coming," someone next to me said.

All these days, despondent and melancholic, I was filled with bitterness, believing neither in myself nor in other people, finding consolation in being harsh toward myself and those close to me.

Vania? He had left and would not return. My presentiment toward him had been realised in reverse: he didn't save me from captivity, rather I saved him from the log. This was all.

Petro Matviyovych, my countryman? What, after all, did he care about me?

I was alone. My friends were lost, my girlfriend never found. I had no family. Eleven years had passed since my father had been shot, six years since I had heard about the death of my mother and my sisters. Nobody would be coming to look for me.

What did I care that these mothers of prisoners had come some three dozen kilometres along impassable roads, across the front lines, where they could have been turned back, arrested, or simply shot. They had been told by Vania or maybe someone else of the whereabouts of their sons.

I could see them approach uncertainly, seeking out their sons, addressing our guard:

"Sir! My son, my son!"

And they came up, flinging themselves into warm embraces, exploding in tears:

"Vitusia! My darling little Viktor!"

The 'Vitusia' was twenty years old, standing at least a metre eighty.

The carefree Viennese remained indifferent. He saw the mothers give their sons food and clothing, and the other prisoners leaned on their shovels as they looked on too, forgetting about the willow and the puddles. The Viennese neither forbade nor allowed. He was beyond feeling, unable to share in the suffering or joy of others. There was not one false note in his irksome whistling.

To which a thought kept being repeated importunately inside my head:

'No one will come to see me!'

63

... These tears! They're as contagious as yawning. I turned and walked away, and fiercely began to hack at the elastic bundle of willow.

I heard someone mention my name and surname. Mine? Maybe it wasn't mine after all. The letters of the surname were transposed.

"Someone's looking for you!" the teacher called me.

I came up. Who could want to see me? An old, tearful woman was trying to read something written on a piece of paper folded umpteen times.

"You...?"

I told her the surname I used then.

She checked.

"Yes, there's a note for you."

Thank you. I took it. And opened it.

The note bore the name of the addressee and only a few words:

> *Your friend came by.*
> *Hold on there. I'll get you out.*
> *Petro Oplenia.*

PASSPORT

1

You probably don't know what you are worth, dear reader. But I know for certain what I am worth: my price is half a kilo of sugar and a bar of soap. For these things, thanks to good people, I was bought out of the prisoner of war camp. This was the price paid for my freedom, my life. A bar of pink soap and half a kilogram of sugar in a white bag.

On December 16th, 1941 I became a free man. I was dressed in a *kufayka*, as the prisoners called it, a torn, wadded army jacket full of parasites. My frozen feet were shod in, or more correctly wrapped in rags tied with string. Several hundred kilometres separated me from my native village. But I was in a far worse predicament when it came to personal papers: to receive a certificate that I had been released from camp, the camp commandant had to be handed a watch or chrome leather boots, or some gold trinket — any one of those things for which a German's honesty, so acclaimed by authors, could be bought.

My countryman, Petro Matviyovych, who had rescued me from the camp, might well have shaken his wallet for me, he might even have given the German a watch to obtain that certificate, but Petro Matviyovych had a wife…

She will probably never forgive him for handing over the sugar (she didn't know about the soap) as part of my ransom.

So I was a free man – hungry, tired, and without money or documents.

Petro Matviyovych brought me home.

Now I had a roof over my head, a warm bed, the worn old shoes of my liberator on my swollen feet, but besides this, no means of support. I couldn't count on finding a job – the town had almost a thousand unemployed teachers alone. And then there were all the accountants, secretaries, book-keepers, and clerks!

I visited the town council several times. Sometimes I was cordially received, sometimes with hostility, but I was not offered work, for to get work one had to have the right connections and influence, and I had only two friends in the whole city: Petro

Matviyovych and Vania. This Red Army soldier had escaped from the camp at the end of November and had not forgotten to bring Petro Matviyovych news of me.

After much searching and begging Petro Matviyovych received a paltry job: to put in order the remains of the city library. In the evening after work, he brought home a heavy yellow lump of an unknown substance. It was called millet bread, which the Germans fed their officials.

Quarrels erupted more and more often in Petro Matviyovych's home, everyone went about hungry, irritable, ready to accept any word as an insult. In the midst of all this I felt myself unwanted, superfluous, and saw myself as the reason for the irritability of his wife and mother-in-law.

But what could I do? Travel home in winter without any warm clothes, with unhealed sores on my feet? It was impossible without a passport.

Books which my good countryman brought home from the library were my only salvation. By reading I could become oblivious to the frightening reality around me, not feel the cold in the room, forget that I was hungry, and not eavesdrop on the women of the house when they were arguing.

Armenians had already opened the first restaurant in the main street, the first professor had already died of hunger and the day after I had finally decided that whatever happened I would begin my trek home, work was finally found for me.

"In five days there will be a general registration of the city's inhabitants," Petro Matviyovych said. "Hanna Denysivna, the wife of Martyn Martynovych, who came to see me yesterday, is in charge of the registry section. I'll chat to him and you'll have a job."

There followed several days of wandering from department to department, notes went from one 'persona' to another, significant whisperings and looks flew in my direction before I became an official of the town council. I was entrusted with – no more, no less – the issue of new German passports to citizens who, for one reason or another, did not have their old Soviet ones.

You simply can't imagine what a fabulous job issuing passports is. Firstly, I nurtured the idea of somehow cooking up a passport for myself. Secondly, I received lunch in the council cafeteria and 200 grammes of bread, and on top of that brought 500 grammes home: 300 for myself, and 200 for Petro Matviyovych's mother-in-law, whom I had been advised to register as my mother.

Thirdly... If the truth be known, the job itself was quite pleasant. Hanna Denysivna, the section supervisor, was somewhere in another room and didn't pay an ounce of attention to me, old Maria Fedorivna transcribed something in one corner, and I could work as I pleased – quickly or slowly, attentively or carelessly.

Ex Red Army soldiers came to me with tattered, crumped pieces of paper, illiterate certificates from enlistment officers stating that their passports had been surrendered. Made-up women looking thirty or more came and assured me that they had lost their passport, and gave their year of birth as 1920 or 1922. Boys who tried to look tough in the streets came in, but became afraid in the office, unable to answer my questions. But mostly they were girls. I ordered them to take their scarves off, examined the shapes of their faces, looked into their eyes, led them to the window and looked again, measured their height and occasionally began to measure them in quite different places to those required, or asked questions which weren't on any of the forms. Some laughed, others blushed, one I remember ran off and returned half an hour later with her *papa*, and then it was my turn to blush.

I observed many different people in those days. There were people with intelligent, aristocratic features, who, in answer to the level of their education replied 'None', and gave 'watchman' as their profession.

There were others who called themselves engineers but who didn't know a word of German nor the Latin alphabet. A woman with flaming red hair stared at me so brazenly that I recorded her as a blonde. A girl with hair combed over her forehead turned bright red when I asked if she had any identifying marks or tattooes. I made her show her arms, but they had nothing. After she had left with her passport, her friend leaned over to me and whispered confidentially:

"She's got the word '*shpana*' tattooed across her forehead. When she was in prison, the *biksas*[21] tattooed her."

People have similar faces and some have very different faces, but when you look deeply into their eyes – they are almost always original and unique.

I had seen all shades of eyes in those days: dark-brown eyes which looked black from a distance, hazel eyes, light hazel, hazel with dark spots or streaks, grey eyes with brown streaks, bicoloured irises with an outer grey ring enclosing a brown ring, yellowish, greenish, grey, dark-grey, dark-grey with a dash of blue, grey-blue and blue-grey, sky blue and cornflower blue. I didn't see any violet eyes, though. Maybe violet eyes are only a figment of poets' imaginations.

But of all the eyes there is one pair I will never forget. A banal phrase? Not quite.

These eyes did not become memorable because of their beauty, for I'm not speaking about the eyes of my sweetheart.

2

My carefree tenure of office as a passport official was suddenly upset by terrible news: Jews were being shot. The Germans were executing Jews.

The supervisor of our section hurried from the commandant to the city council, then to the police station, and from there to the registration points.

The commandant's office demanded lists of Jews from her, but she didn't have them and couldn't have had them, for the question of nationality had not been forseen when it was decided to register the populace.

After the horror, the absurdly cruel treatment, the blind brutality I had seen and endured as a prisoner, I had to believe in this most horrible news – and yet I lacked the strength to believe. One day I bumped into Vania, my friend from the camp. He told me how his neighbour, a Jewish doctor, had been taken away, how the wife had fainted on the doorstep, how the twelve-year-old daughter had

---

[21] *Biksa* – underworld term for 'whore'.

68

appeared at night barefoot, her eye torn out by a bullet and dangling on a thread. In the morning she was taken away again to be finished off.

The question concerned the total annihilation of a nation.

If in the late Middle Ages and the Rennaissance period, in the times of so-called confessional thought, people found it necessary to send the adherents of other religions into the other world, if in our times the builders of Marx's class socialism did not stop at destroying several classes of society, then these builders of national socialism would probably not hesitate to destroy an entire nation.

People who think in terms of class, position, religion, tribe, and race – aren't they only seeking a scapegoat for their hatred? And aren't all such incidents a manifestation of a dark animal instinct, a primeval thirst for killing buried deep within all of us?

These were my thoughts when I was returning from Vania's place.

Goose down was flying about in the street. An empty Jewish apartment was being ransacked and someone had torn open a pillow. I was stopped by gendarmes on the corner and asked to show my 'Ausweis'. I showed them the certificate I was issued with at work, printed in Russian and German. I was asked if I was a Jew. I replied, certainly not, and was sent on my way.

Hanna Denysivna began to watch my work closely. When the author Lohvytsky came in, a man with very Semitic features, she forbade me to issue him a passport, and told him that even though he had all the necessary papers, he would have to bring along two witnesses who could swear that he was not Jewish.

I regretted that I hadn't made out a passport for myself before. Now it was much harder to do so.

One morning Hanna Denysivna called for me.

"Can you remember if there were many Jewish-looking people in the first days that you were issuing passports."

I made the indiscretion of saying:

"No, only two or three."

She looked at me in fright.

"That's horrible! We'll be shot! You must look through the files at once and make a list of all the Jews."

I found the names of several people whom I knew for certain were not Jewish and gave them to her. She sent old Maria Fedorivna, the secretary, to check on their nationality. Poor Maria Fedorivna tramped for hours through the fresh snow of empty streets seeking the alleged Jews, and so they wouldn't suspect, pretended to fill in some unanswered questions on the forms. At the end of the day she brought good tidings – there was not a single Jew among the suspected people. I already knew that, without her confirmation.

The next day Hanna Denysivna again called me in for a secret talk. My supervisor was even more afraid and secretive than the day before.

"A girl will come round today. Her surname is Vasilieva. Her father is Russian, fighting somewhere at the front now. Her mother was Jewish and she's been shot. I've told you before, that according to the commandant's office, a Jew is anyone having a quarter or more Jewish blood in them. So when this Vasilieva comes to see you, you must write in her passport that she's Jewish."

I said all right, and returned to my desk. It's my nature to agree to everything and then do things my own way. I didn't hesitate for a minute, and didn't even ask myself whom I should listen to: my own conscience or Hanna Denysivna.

When this Vasilieva arrived, I had to register her as a Russian, Ukrainian, Pole, or Armenian — anything but a Jew.

The best thing would have been if Hanna Denysivna had gone somewhere on business and left me the stamp, as she had done on occasions. I would have had a free hand. But to my sorrow and disappointment, Hanna Denysivna didn't prepare to go anywhere. I began working on various strategies which would help me to save the girl.

Perhaps I should write her out a passport in any old name, make Vasilieva into Vorobyova? But she might not understand and could protest, asking why? Then at best, my intention would come to nothing.

It was close on eleven when she came. Though I had never seen her before, and didn't watch her as she came up to my desk, I could sense with all my being that it was her, the girl whose fate rested in my hands, the girl I was to save or condemn. For the word '*Judin*' in her passport would mean nothing less than a death sentence.

She offered me her papers. I looked up at her: a hand with long fingers unaccustomed to physical work, a tall, almost childish figure, face pale as if after a long illness, large grey-blue eyes.

She was smiling.

There was not one Semitic feature in her whole appearance. I accepted her papers. A certificate from the housing administrator, a report that she had finished eight grades of school, her birth certificate. In the birth certificate it had: Irina Vasilieva, father Vasyl Petrovich, mother Hilda Aronivna.

Yes.

I tore a sheet from an exercise book and wrote in large letters: 'I'll write in your passport that you are Voro...' At this moment I felt someone's intent gaze upon me. And it wasn't the girl's. I looked up and met Hanna Denysivna's eyes. She was in the doorway of her office, pointing at the girl with her eyes and noiselessly mouthing the words 'that's her', and made some signs which I didn't understand.

Hanna Denysivna, no doubt knew the girl personally. My plan to make her Vorobyova had fallen through. The blood rushed to my head, hammering at my temples, but I controlled myself and calmed down. The girl before me was a good example; several days ago she had lost her mother, she didn't know what the future held, and yet she looked calm, even joyful.

A strong-willed person smiles at his own suffering.

Slowly I filled out the forms and finally reached the passport. I took her over to the wall to measure her height, looked at her blonde hair, peered into her blue eyes, doing everything seriously for the first time. At first she smiled at me, but then noticing my sullen looks, stopped. She wasn't interested in what I was writing, and studied the ink-well, the table, Maria Fedorivna, my shorn head.

Suddenly a new thought flashed through my mind. Not to write anything for her nationality. Maybe Hanna Denysivna wouldn't notice and would affix the stamp. But Hanna Denysivna was watching my every move.

"Remember what I said!" her voice rang out.

71

I remembered that Hanna Denysivna was a teacher by profession and had told me several days earlier of her ability to read a pen's movements, just as we read letters.

And so I wrote: 'Judin'.

The girl was staring at the floor.

I made her sign in a book, then handed her the dreadful passport for her signature.

She signed without looking at the line containing her death sentence. Then the supervisor confirmed the sentence with her stamp and I issued the new passport to its owner.

Again I looked into the girl's eyes. She understood nothing. I wanted her to protest, to scream, to throw the passport in my face, but she only placed it in her pocket, gave me a meek, affable smile and left, saying goodbye.

3

The best way to calm down, to allay the voice of conscience, is to blame yourself vehemently, to let your conscience blast away with all its might and fury.

Then it will quickly tire and fall asleep.

Returning home from work I chastised myself for being a weak-willed fool and a coward. I should have refused to issue her with a passport. But what would that have achieved? Maria Fedorivna would have issued the passport instead of me and nothing would have changed. And I could have been fired from the job and lost my 500 grammes of bread and the possibility of getting a passport for myself.

No, this was not the way to think. The most shameful excuse was to say: 'If I don't do it, someone else will.'

… Why hadn't I asked her about her nationality, as I had done with the others? Had I lacked the strength?

Yet I had the strength to write stealthily, sneakily, basely, that she was Jewish.

At home, after tea and millet bread, I dived into a book to escape the terrible reality. I sought authors whose works were not a reflection of reality, but a dreamed up, invented, fairy-tale world, which existed only inside the author's mind. In his one and a half months as librarian, my landlord had brought home over a hundred books, so I had something to choose from. I grabbed Sologub, who had said of himself: 'I take a piece of life, dirty and grey, and mould it into a sweet legend, for I am a poet.'

I was holding a copy of the poems of Sologub[22].

I let the book fall open itself, and began to read what my eyes fell on first, the last lines of a poem:

> *Though you may die yourself,*
> *Save the one who calls out to you!*

Familiar grey-blue eyes looked at me and I knew at once what I needed to do. I read the entire poem, softly repeated the last two lines, and said in a low voice: "I must rescue her, even at the price of my own life."

"What?" Petro Matviyovych's wife asked from the next room.

"I'm off to Vania's place. I'll spend the night there," I replied.

"But it's late, it's a quarter to six. You won't make it. There's a curfew after six."

"It's all right, I'll make it."

I was right to go to Vania's. Again he related to me the last minutes of the Jewish street near which he lived.

"You know what old Surka said to me the day before she was taken away? 'If this dog Hitler was to lick my heart he'd die, it's so bitter'."

... "Why didn't they leave?" Vania asked sadly. "Surely they knew what awaited them?"

"There were many enemies of Bolshevism among the old pre-revolutionary Jewish intelligentsia. And the poor just didn't have the means to leave."

"But now, when some are being taken away, the others sit at home and wait till they come for them. The fools should run or hide."

"They believe, Vania, it will passs them by. Weak-spirited people always hope for the best. They become optimists, because they haven't the strength to acknowledge the ghastly truth. You ask

---

[22] Fedor Sologub (1863-1927), born Fedor Teternikov, a Russian symbolist poet, novelist, translator, playwright and essayist.

why they don't hide? But who would take them in? Some rejoice at their death, others are afraid to shelter them. Would you take someone in, for instance?"

Vania looked into my eyes, mulling something over. Then he leaned forward and grinned:

"A Jewish woman slept here the other night."

"Young?"

"Ah, young! She was forty-five at the very least."

Now it was my turn to lean forward. With a 'Listen, Vania!' I began to recount the story of the terrible passport.

"So," I finished, "you and I need to save this girl."

"Alright, I'll take her in for a few days, but no more, because..."

"No, I'm not talking about hiding her. Listen. I issue passports to ex-Soviet soldiers on the production of a certificate from the enlistment office. These are usually untyped, written in indelible pencil on scraps of paper. They often look very suspicious, but no one checks the authenticity of the stamps on them except me. I record the number of the certificate and return it to the owner with a mark showing that a passport has been issued. So I risk nothing in issuing a passport under a false certificate. Understand? We'll write you out a certificate now, stamp it with a five-copeck coin, and tomorrow you'll come to me at work and we'll make her a passport. We'll give you a name which is both male and female. Aleksandr, for example, and by adding a letter at the end we'll have Aleksandra."

Vania jumped about the room and caught me in his arms.

"Don't rejoice yet," I told him, "it's not that easy to do. A thousand unforseen obstacles may still lie in our way."

4

In fact there were enough obstacles.

As soon as I had arrived in the office, the supervisor sternly warned me not to issue passports to anyone not registered with the employment bureau. This regulation had been in force from the very beginning, but I hadn't adhered to it very strictly. Especially when beautiful girls came in. It was a pity to send them to the

74

employment bureau, where there was always a large crowd and one didn't know why one had to waste the day there.

Vania came at half past nine as agreed. As if on purpose a crowd of people had turned up. I had just begun to write out a passport for a deaf and illiterate stupid old woman. Her papers were torn and frayed and could not be read, so I had to ask her everything, and she either didn't know, didn't hear, or didn't understand.

I had to fix Vania up with a passport as soon as possible. The girl could be arrested at any moment. I took Vania's certificate out of turn after finishing with the old woman.

A gold-toothed man protested from the head of the queue:

"Eh, why are you pushing in? You mug!"

Hanna Denysivna swam out of her office at the disturbance. She took Vania's certificate from me, written in my handwriting and bearing a forged stamp. I must have turned white.

She turned to Vania:

"Where's the employment bureau stamp? Go immediately and register with the bureau and don't upset our procedures." Then she turned to me:

"What did I tell you? Not to register anyone without a reference from the employment bureau. Don't introduce your own rules here."

The insolent gold-toothed character placed his papers before me with a victorious look on his face.

Holding onto the certificate, Vania darted past the queue and disappeared.

Our plans had fallen through.

It was seven past twelve. Maria Fedorivna, the secretary, had left for lunch. Hanna Denysivna was locking her desk and preparing to go to lunch. I wanted to wait her out. Maybe she might forget to lock up the passport blanks, and I could try to sneak a couple. One for me, the other for the Jewish girl.

Suddenly the door flew open and in burst Vania. He was breathing heavily, his face red and sweaty. His coat was torn at the sleeve, with several buttons missing.

"Here... is the... employment... bureau stamp," he gasped.

75

"We are closed now. Come back at two," Hanna Denysivna said.

I began to implore her:

"Hanna Denysivna! I'll write it out for him now. Why should he come a second time."

"Don't set down your own rules here. Go to lunch. I'm locking the office."

When I finally began on Vania's passport, the unexpected happened again. An acquaintance of Vania's appeared.

"Ah, Vania, you here too. Well, how are things? Waiting for your passport? But you've come to the wrong place. You don't get yours here, do you? This is the central registration point for the city centre. You live near Chortoplakhivka, so you'd have to go to point 'D'."

Fortunately, Hanna Denysivna overheard nothing. I sat engrossed in my paperwork, acting as if I had heard nothing either. My heart thumped anxiously: this character would probably want to see Vania's new passport. I had to get rid of him.

I lifted my head and asked him:

"What business are you here on?"

"I need a passport for my daughter. She's sick in bed at the moment, so could you issue one without her being present. I'll give you all the details."

"Bring a doctor's certificate to show that she is sick and then we'll write one out. A note from the apartment administrator will do."

I thought the situation had been saved, that he'd run off to his doctor, but no, he approached Vania again and talked, and talked...

Sliding Vania's passport under some papers, I rewrote some useless information. My indignation grew and grew. I raised my head a second time:

"Excuse me, you're disturbing me. Go to your doctor, and hurry, because we close at four and you won't make it."

A lengthy appeal to forgive him, a lengthy farewell to Vania, and the character disappeared.

At last everything was ready.

Trying to look calm and nonchalant I walked up to Hanna Denysivna for the stamp. I'm interested to know what I looked like then, whether I gave myself away, whether I was in full control, whether anyone could notice what was going on inside me.

I only saw that Hanna Denysivna noticed nothing. She took the passport from me to look through it. What if she had thought of checking the description in the passport with the features of Vania, who was sitting near the open doors of the registration room?

What would have resulted? Vania was tall, had a round face, dark hair, and hazel eyes. But in the passport it said: height average, face oval, hair light blond, eyes grey-blue.

Hanna Denysivna lay the passport on the table and applied the stamp. The stamp was pale and upside down. Hanna Denysivna intently poured ink onto the stamp pad, pressed the stamp on it firmly and stamped the passport energetically a second time. The two imprints merged together and nothing could be made out on the paper. My supervisor thought for a long time and said quietly:

"Write him out another passport. This one's no good."

I sat down to write out another passport. A voice screamed inside me: faster, faster!

At last the passport was ready, and the stamp affixed.

I took it over to my desk and hurriedly made alterations: 'Aleksandr' to 'Aleksandra', 'Russe' to 'Russin', from a 1915 date of birth to 1925. Maria Fedorivna looked on incredulously at what I was doing. Let her. I gave Vania the passport and said softly:

"Wait for me in the street. I'll be out in a minute."

Maria Fedorivna overheard me and asked:

"He a friend?"

"Yes," I said and addressed Hanna Denysivna:

"I need to go somewhere now. I'll be back in half an hour."

The answer was what I had expected:

"No running around in office hours!"

"Then I'm leaving without your permission."

Vania and I were standing in a large apartment block outside room eight. She lived here, the girl with the grey-blue eyes. No, maybe she had lived here, for the door was locked and no one answered. Maybe she was afraid to open it? Maybe she was out?

Maybe she had run away and hidden in someone's place?

But neither of us dared utter the last 'maybe': maybe she had met her mother's fate.

We knocked on the neighbour's door. A dishevelled barefoot woman answered it. I said to her:

"We are city council officials. We must see Irina Vasilieva. Could you tell us where we can find her?"

"Go to the Clay Pit, you'll find her there..." The door banged shut.

"Vania, where's the Clay Pit?"

"On the outskirts of town, where the Germans execute the Jews."

To substantiate the news we asked the other neighbour. She told us everything. How Irina's mother had been arrested, how the girl had cried, how she had become fearful yesterday when she read at home in her passport that she was registered as being Jewish. And today, no more than an hour ago, German gendarmes had come and taken her away. She probably wouldn't be returning.

I didn't go back to my place of work. In the fatally late passport I again changed Aleksandra to Aleksandr, 1925 to 1915 and Russin to Russe, hid the passport in my pocket, filled a bag with a day's ration of bread and some crusts from Vania, threw in Sologub's book of poetry, thanked Petro Matviyovych and his family, said goodbye to Vania and set out west to venture along the endless roads with my ailing feet.

THE ESCAPE

1

Death was staring at me with two black eyes. I didn't say 'a pair of eyes' intentionally, but 'two eyes'. These eyes didn't belong to the same person, and yet all the same they belonged to him. The first one, immobile, was further away and higher up than the second, which was closer and kept oscillating back and forth. The upper eye belonged to a man with a dirty ribbon tied diagonally across his face, under which, if it existed, was concealed his other eye. The lower eye was the muzzle of an automatic pistol. Other than that, there was no great difference between the two. Both were round and black, both spelled death.

"You scum of the earth, why are you crawling around here? Why aren't you at the front?" the owner of the pistol hissed at me.

I stood before him with my hands in the air, not knowing what to say. I wanted very much to kick him in the groin. Then it would become clear what I should do. But behind him stood three more armed characters. The worst thing was that I didn't know who they were. They obviously looked as if they had power, but they didn't appear to belong to the new administration, or the police, for these wouldn't have asked why I wasn't at the front. Without knocking or excusing themselves they barged into the house whose occupants had put me up for the night. They asked to be fed and then directed their attention at me. The minute they learned that I wasn't the people's son, but only a passing traveller, I saw a pistol dancing before me in drunken hands.

"Which front you from?" I asked foolishly to win time and work out just what lies I had to spin.

"Goddamn! Don't you know the front?" the character with one eye hissed.

"Leave 'im alone. Can't you see the fellow's scared shitless," said one of the men standing at the back, and coarsely added what would happen to my pants as a result of my fear. The others roared with laughter.

I took this for a good omen and lowered my hands. The one-eyed character waved his pistol about again, but a tall bearded fellow beside him asked civilly:

"Have you got any documents?"

I pulled out my passport where it stated that I was Aleksandr Vasiliev, Russian, born 1915 – the same passport which was to have saved the life of another person, but now might save mine. The passport created some interest. None of the characters knew much German so I had to translate for them. Suddenly the short red-haired fellow at the back had an idea:

"Boys! He's a spy!" he said, pointing at me. "Where could an ordinary person have obtained a German passport? He's a spy all right, and he speaks German too."

"Take a closer look," I replied. "This passport is as much mine as it is yours," and I pointed to the corrected places. "See, it's forged."

After a short interrogation about who I was, where I was from, where I was going, whether I'd been in the army, and so on, the tall fellow ordered:

"You'll come with us!"

I had previously heard nothing about Soviet partisans. Judging by the appearance of these armed men dressed in semi-military garb, I had taken them for the remains of a unit routed by the Germans and fighting its way back east. I replied with silence which was taken as a sign of agreement.

And so I found myself in a 'unit commanded by comrade Fedorov'. The unit was to become a division, but for the moment consisted of commandants and commissars, the command staff, a radio operator, a doctor, and thirty chance travellers like me. I moved with the detachment for eight days. I saw a live German being skinned, and later a hundred innocent villagers from nearby were shot in revenge. I saw them find a German soldier frozen solid. His feet and the fingers of his hand were chopped off and taken into the house to thaw out, so they could take the boots off the feet and the gold rings off his fingers. I saw three people like me executed: boys returning home from concentration camps or seiges. Two were executed for refusing to join the detachment, saying that they had fought their war and wanted to return home as soon as possible. Another was shot after he had agreed to join and then tried to escape.

Luckily I wasn't entrusted with any executions. The chief of staff made me an interpreter and a military clerk (without paper or office), and placed me in charge of cultural education. The best thing was that I was exempted from duty detail. Quite unexpectedly I was offered the easiest and simplest way of getting medals, fame, and an opportunity to legalise my dubious social status in Soviet society. I could have...

When I saw the body of the fellow killed for trying to escape, I told myself that I had to escape that night, but in such a way that my escape would avenge the three shot in my presence, the unknown numbers they had shot before, and those they would execute in the future.

I have never had to kill a person. That doesn't mean that I'm against killing as such, that I'm against killing under any circumstances. No, not at all. There were several times in my life when it was worth killing, when I should have killed, where I certainly needed to kill. There were times when I raised a gun in defence of someone else's honour or my own life, but I have never killed anyone. Even after a friend and I left one lecher lying on the road with a cracked skull, we learned a sometime later that the 'victim' had survived and been discharged from hospital. Another time I raced up to my pursuer who had spent all his cartridges on me, and the bullet of his partner, who was doubtless aiming at me, laid him dead at my feet.

But this time I was certain I would kill.

2

Fedorov slept very soundly, the sleep of a tired and drunk person. We slept without undressing, only taking our shoes off and undoing every possible button. First I did up every button I had, then did my belt up, found my cold quilted jacket among the warm things of the others which covered me. There was still the footwear. I wasn't too careful about being quiet – if the fellow woke up, all the better. The automatic weapon was closer to me than to him.

Beside the stove stood his new boots and my old shoes, two sizes too big for me. I put on his boots. The axe lay here near the stove, between two logs. I had chopped wood the day before on purpose, and instead of returning the axe to the people who had put us up, I hid it among the logs.

I looked around to see if anyone was watching and took the axe. It was blunt and notched in two places. Maybe it'd be better to hit him with the butt end.

Stepping boldly forward I approached the bed. As a future commander it was beneath his dignity to sleep on the floor with the rest of us. I did not hurry — fear usually compels people to act hastily, but I had nothing to fear: the owners were asleep in the next room, red-headed Sienka was on guard duty and would return in about an hour and a half. And as for this fellow, his business was settled.

I stood over him. The oblique light of the moon caught the edge of his pillow and reflected from it like a thin spurt of water from a hard surface, disintegrating into myriads of tiny specks of light. Next to this fountain of light, faintly lit by its outermost splashes, lay the dark shape of a heavy dishevelled head. It had sunk deep into the pillow, as if it had been pushed into it. The hard, wiry stubble of the unshaven face pierced the fine linen.

How could I hit him so that the blood wouldn't splash onto my face or clothes?

I chose a more comfortable position, to be able to unwind for the blow, gripped the handle with both hands and unexpectedly noticed that my right hand wanted to make the sign of the cross. How odd! I hadn't crossed myself for maybe ten years. Why the sudden urge now?

Now or after? Better after…

I swung the axe back for a better strike and realised suddenly that to axe a sleeping man to death was not the same as killing someone who is attacking you or at least defending himself. Surprisingly, I felt I wanted to avert the blow, as if it wasn't me about to make the blow, but someone aiming at me. When someone walks across the ice and falls through unexpectedly before your eyes, you grab at the air with your hands to stop yourself from falling, and you feel a sharp pain as if your legs had been immersed

82

in icy water. Or if three steps in front of you a car travelling at maddening speed slices into a pedestrian, the reaction is to scream and close one's eyes, unable to comprehend whose life is ending at that moment.

... I took a step back and caught myself picturing the figure of Raskolnikov from a watercolour by Karazin I had once seen: Raskolnikov at the moment of murder, axe bloodied. But why all this now? What had I in common with Raskolnikov? Only perhaps that both of us were wielding the same weapon. But apart from that...

Raskolnikov vacillated, agonised, attempted to kill while I suffered no doubts while planning my attack, and would carry out what I had decided with the same ease that this black-haired commander had chopped off the legs and fingers of the frozen German. I raised the axe a second time and again felt as if someone wouldn't allow me to do what I wanted. Ever since childhood I have noticed some alien force inside me which surfaced only at crucial moments in my life; occasionally it pushed me toward some action or other, sometimes it held me back, but each time I had full control over myself and it, always I was stronger than it. I would overcome this force now too, only... only how good it would be if he woke up! If he could at least see his death, understand the reason for it. Should I wake him?

But maybe then I'd have even less resolve to carry out my plan? For I'd see before me the eyes of a man with whom, despite our differences, I had eaten bread and drunk vodka; a man who had treated me better than the others though he had not been better than them.

I stood more comfortably, to strike with full force, and carefully moved the chair away from the bed. I did this carefully and was surprised at myself. Why the caution? I'm supposed to be indifferent as to whether they hear me or not. I fixed my hands around the axe handle once more. Unplaned and rough, it had given me blisters while I was chopping wood. Maybe I should wrap my hands in a handkerchief so as not to break my blisters? But enough thinking. I had been standing over him for several minutes, unable to strike. If only Sienka had returned unexpectedly, then I'd have to fight two men; it would have given me resolve. Besides, Sienka was an animal and it would have been easier to begin with him.

* * *

I replaced the axe in its place and walked over to the door. When I touched the door latch the bed springs creaked behind me and something moved and muttered a few syllables... 'He's woken up!' I realised, and the realisation contained fear, pity, and joy. I rushed up to the bed unarmed... No, he had only turned his head, straightened his arm, and was sleeping just as soundly as before. Suddenly I was seized by a burning anger at myself, at my powerlessness, and at him, lying there as if charmed against harm.

Calmly and resolutely I went over to the stove and got the axe. Two more steps, and I was beside the bed. The moonlight had disappeared. I must have spent quite some time standing there deliberating. Again, just like the first time, an invisible hand held my raised axe back. Where had it come from, this unknown force? I was reminded of the first time that I dived into a river from a high bank. The bank was clayey, eroded, and there was nothing unusual about it. But when I stepped to the edge to dive in as my friends had done, I found an unknown force acting there, which wouldn't let me take the final, decisive step. Then I overcame the force quite easily, perhaps because I was afraid of looking foolish before my friends. Now the same or similar force, the existence of which I had no knowledge of even fifteen minutes before, appeared hard, strong, unyielding.

No, I really couldn't kill a sleeping man. I did not and could not execute my plan.

I went outside onto the porch. The front-door latch burned my hand with icy metal. The moon was perched atop the distant forest, its light already tarnished and dull, growing weaker by the minute.

I steered a straight course through vegetable plots along the same dog track toward the setting moon. It was hard going, maybe because I kept sinking into the snow, or because I felt broken, destroyed, unworthy of the opinion I had of myself. My own will had betrayed me, and this was worse than a sweetheart's betrayal. I knew it wasn't physical fatigue pressing down on me, bending me to the ground: unsaid words and unfinished actions weigh heavily upon one's conscience.

SOKHACHOVKA

1

The road sign said: *Sochatschowka 17 km.*

Sokhachovka.

I continued without slowing down, but my thoughts revolved around the word 'Sokhachovka'. When and where had I heard the name? It was my first time in the locality, I didn't have a map with me, nor had I ever looked at a map and remembered such a trifling name as Sokhachovka. Maybe there was another Sokhachovka, apart from the one I had once heard about? Back home there was no village or town by that name. And during my protracted wanderings I don't remember having come across a single Sokhachovka. Perhaps it was mentioned in the works of some author? Unlikely.

But why then was the word so strangly familiar? And why did it reek of something abominable, unspeakably repugnant, as if it bore the stench of decomposing bodies?

Perhaps I was just emotionally drained, my nerves on edge, having been on the run for two weeks now, evading Soviet partisans and German gendarmes, perplexed at the dilemma facing me: to avoid the Germans meant trekking through marshes and forests crawling with partisans, and to avoid falling into partisan hands, I had to choose major roads and towns where Germans hunted down people like me.

I knew that nervous people often imagined they were reliving a past experience. So I too had probably never been here before, had never seen the roadsign or read what was written on it.

Such reflections helped to put my mind at ease and forget this damned Sokhachovka.

I took a good look around.

Snow, snow, snow everywhere.

A grey forest on the horizon. The road was nearing a village. The kit-bag cut into my shoulder, my blistered and frozen feet were hurting, my fingers were blue with cold and would not bend, and the prickly cold filtered in through the tear on my knee where I had

86

fallen the day before and torn my pants, gradually making my right leg turn completely numb.

The feeling of hunger was not too strong. I could fight it, I could force myself to ignore it. However, the feeling of fatigue was growing, and becoming all encompassing: it was becoming ever harder to fight it off.

It was a pity that I had abandoned my thoughts on whether I had known about the existence of Sokhachovka before.

The village lay before me.

Actually what lay before me didn't at all resemble a village in the Ukrainian sense of the word. I remembered our villages from distant childhood. Yards fenced in or bordered with trees, with a cattle-shed always coming out onto the street; inside the yards were wells with the immutable shadoof; the houses blinding white in spring and summer, in winter blanketed with moss or surrounded with reeds; tall threshing barns; willows with countless crows' nests; orchards a cloud of pale pink smoke in spring, with the silky rustle of leaves in summer, and in winter covered with silver flecks of hoarfrost.

What I had previously called a village looked nothing like this. There were houses scattered along the road, occasionally a tiny cattle-shed resting against a house, stuck together from bits of board and reeds. Not one barn, no sign of any fences. Everything bore the stamp of neglect, decline, doom.

A real Russian *derevnia*.

Far away, in the middle of the wide street, several women stood gossiping.

I made for them, though I knew from personal experience that it was useless asking people one met in the street where one could spend the night or get some food. The answer was a standard: 'No one's died on the road here yet! Just go into any house, the people will take you in and feed you.'

No one will ever say: 'Come with me.'

It's no use even trying to find out just which house one should go to.

Enter the nearest house. Six or eight frightened children stare at you, eyes and mouths wide open, the eldest only twelve or so.

Don't even try to find out where their mama is.

In the next house the door is locked; loud voices can be heard inside. At one's knocking a face appears in the window and disappears even faster than it appeared. Don't knock any more, they won't open up.

Further on, an amazingly neat, wealthy house. Roomy and sunny inside. You are met at the door by a friendly, understanding man. 'As you can see for yourself,' he says, 'there's nowhere for you to spend the night.' And as for food, they've nothing to eat themselves. He's really very sorry for poor wretches like you, but how can he help? You agree with him and move on.

In the next house the fellow has sly eyes and a cunning smile. He begins by interrogating you: 'So, then, brother, you never wanted to fight for the Soviets and you're running from the Germans? Know what happens to people like you? Germans came upon three like you recently, took them outside the village and shot them. They're still lying there. You'll see them as you leave'. At these words he is all smiles, as if he's telling you about some joyous event.

After you have lost count of the houses visited, you will be humanely taken in. You can stay the night there, though you'll have to sleep on the floor, but that's alright, they'll bring some straw in. Food? Sit down, sit down. There's food, though it mightn't be what you're used to at home. You eat from a suspiciously dirty bowl with an obviously dirty spoon and notice someone groaning on a bed in a dark corner.

You ask who it is and what's the matter, is he sick?

Yes. He's their eldest son, a grown lad. He's very ill. Spotted fever.

So wandering from house to house was unpleasant, humiliating, and almost as fruitless as asking people in the street. Maybe to win five minutes, to delay my begging for five minutes, I went past the first dwellings towards the women assembled in the street.

There were three of them.

One was balancing a yoke hung with full heavy buckets on her shoulders. The second woman's buckets were on the ground and she was leaning on her curved yoke. The third, young and tall, had nothing with her and was dressed in city clothes.

Seeing the tall teacher (who else could she have been) in city dress I felt joyous and carefree for some inexplicable reason, as if I had met someone near and dear to me.

I couldn't see their faces. Two were standing with their backs to me and shielded the third from my view.

When I approached the women, all three stopped their noisy conversation as if on command and turned toward me.

The oldest, a broad-backed grandma with the yoke on her shoulders had no nose, not even a sign that such a part of her anatomy had ever existed. The second woman's sooty-grey face had something resembling a raspberry button which had been twisted to one side and flattened.

The face of the third, the young one, whom I took for a teacher, was hidden under bandages, revealing only her mouth and eyes. I felt a twist of disgust rise deep within my tired body.

It was too late to walk past the women as if they didn't exist. I had headed straight for them. Besides, it was too late to turn off into the nearest yard.

I came up and greeted them with my usual question: where could I get a meal and spend the night.

"Marisha here will take you into the schoolhouse. Won't you, Marisha?"

The teacher, her identity now confirmed, looked at me through her bandages.

"Have you got many lice? I took one bugger in recently and the bastard infested the whole bed with lice."

Despite the coarseness of the words, her voice breathed at me with the unexpected warmth of a forgotten past, as if something had flared up suddenly and then died away. Where had I heard this voice? Or whose voice did it remind me of?

"He's not bad looking," said the woman with a crimson button for a nose, looking me up and down. "Where ya from?"

"The front line."

"Going far?"

"Back home to Ukraine."

"So you're from Ukraine?" the teacher asked unexpectedly in Ukrainian. "A countryman must be put up for the night." And then reverting to Russian: "Wait here, I'll run and get some milk."

89

Sparkling eyes looked at me kindly, beautifully traced lips smiled at me. Through the bandages... I nodded in agreement.

Quickly and gracefully she turned on her left heel and ran off.

And then I recognised her. By the movement, by this quick turn. But I didn't run after her, I didn't shout 'Marusia!'. I lowered my eyes so the intensity of my gaze would not make her look back. Because now, after I had recognised her, she would have recognised me too.

The woman with no sign of a nose chattered away:

"Eh, how she runs! The *khakhlushka*[23]. Been in our village almost five years. Ah, but she loves the men... All the prisoners come to her to stay the night."

"She's entices all the men," the second added.

"And she can really sing too!" the first put in again.

The door of the peeling grey house Marusia had disappeared into slammed shut. I had to escape as soon as possible, before she could see me. I asked:

"What's your *derevnia* called?"

The old women replied together: 'Mitriukhina' or 'Petriukhina', I didn't quite catch what they had said.

"Hey, I've come to the wrong place then. I need to be in Deriuhina." (Deriuhina was the *derevnia* I had passed through several hours earlier.)

"Stay the night at Marisha's. Where will you go?"

"But a friend's waiting for me in Deriuhina. How do I get there?"

I was shown the road along which I had just come. Thanking them, I walked away as fast as I could.

A door slammed behind me. That was probably Marusia coming out. My heart quivered, I felt as if someone had me by the shoulder and was forcibly turning my face in her direction. But I fought the invisible hand and step by step moved further and further away, staring at the ground.

Don't look back, just don't look back!

---

[23] Derogatory Russian term for Ukrainian women.

2

In the spring of 1936 I lived in... it could have been Voronezh, or perhaps Orel, or Briansk – it's not all that important. The room I rented was far from the town centre on a quiet street lined with small idyllic buildings fenced in grey and shaded by clusters of flowering lilac. The street was rutted by rain and quite impassable to any sort of traffic, green and dreamily sunny during the day, at night fragrant with the smell of flowers and the nightingale's song.

One Sunday I came up to the window to shave. The sun's blinding light bounced off the mirror into my eyes, and then I turned the mirror onto the wall of the green three-windowed house across the street. Now I had the key with which I could unlock the secrets of what was happening in that strange house, and I began to run the beam of light over the windows.

Anyone aged nineteen would have done the same.

In the first window I noticed nothing interesting, a cupboard at the back of the room, a large framed painting on the wall. I moved my projector to the second window. It rested on a beautiful girl's face. The blonde girl, no older than seventeen, was sitting on a bed reading. She closed her eyes and hid behind the book from the blinding light.

I lay the mirror down, but a minute later (I repeat, I was only nineteen) I removed the large heavy mirror from the wall and aimed a blinding shaft of light at the window beyond which the girl sat. She stood up, I hid lightning fast, jumping to one side and thinking that she hadn't seen me. A few minutes later when I looked again I could see no one through the open window.

I sat down to shave, then went off to town and returned late in the afternoon.

Just before sunset I was sitting by the window reading. Suddenly a bright patch of light fell on my book. I looked up and was blinded by an explosion of reflected sunlight. Yellow and green spots danced before my eyes, but I still looked stubbornly in the direction of the light, and though red spots joined the yellow and green ones, I managed to see a white hand holding a hand-mirror and a smiling young face. Eye for an eye, tooth for a tooth! She was repaying me for my morning escapade.

That was the beginning of our quaint friendship.

Not a word passed between us. The street was wide and you wouldn't scream: 'Hi! What's! your! name!!!'

Any other time I would probably have been more enthusiastic about establishing a real relationship, but I liked the uniqueness of this friendship with its romantic overtones. Our sunlight conversations continued, a playful exchange of light. In the mornings before she disappeared I pursued her with the mirror, and in the late afternoon when the sun fell on her windows she pursued me.

May was ending, the lilac was shedding its flowers onto the secluded street, the jasmine was flowering. I wanted to write poems, I wanted to remember, no not remember, but to experience spring with all my heart and hold it inside me forever.

One evening I was returning home after visiting my countryman, Petro Matviyovych Oplenia, whom I bumped into by chance in the street. Actually he was a little afraid when I recognised him. I called out his name and he approached with the words: 'What do you want?'

He couldn't have recognised me. He had last seen me when I was twelve. I identified myself and told him where I was from. He mumbled and stuttered:

"You're mistaken, I'm not the person you think I am."

I did not relent: "But I'm the son of so and so."

He couldn't stand it any longer and asked: "Where's your father?"

We went to his apartment and told each other our stories — the usual stories of dispossessed peasants and their children. Five years later this meeting proved very useful: my countryman bought me my freedom from a prisoner-of-war camp. But back then, at the end of May 1936, I took away from this meeting with a person I had not seen for seven years only an even stronger lyrical frame of mind.

Approaching my lodgings, I heard singing. I was so engrossed in childhood reminiscences swaddled in mists of time, that I didn't notice a strange thing: the song was ours, Ukrainian, and didn't seem possible to come from anywhere in this Russian land. I was at my door by the time the song had finished and looked in the direction from which it had come. A window in the green building was open, the same window where my friendly stranger lived. I could sense a female form in the room; she came forward, all in white, sat on the windowsill and began again:

"Where the Yatran twists and turns..."

Music has an irresistible, magnetic attraction for me and, hardly thinking what I was doing, I was drawn toward my magnet. Actually I didn't walk, but crawled, because to cross the so-called street I had to descend into a water-worn gully, which was also used as a clay pit and a refuse dump, and then clamber up the other side.

She was called Marusia.

Like me she was a 'fragment of an exploded whole'. Like me, she had no one left in the world. She aspired to become an actress, a singer, but this was only a dream; at present she was a finals student at the pedagogical technical school. She lived off her scholarship of sixty roubles a month, although she made a bit on the side by sewing. But now she had no time for that. Her exams were coming. She had to study to be one of the two lucky ones from her year who would be allowed to continue their studies without having to spend two years in the field. It was said that it was only two years, but in actual fact almost none of the teachers sent to the remote villages ever had the chance to escape and enter a tertiary institution.

During the following days, while Marusia was preparing for exams, I stole half an hour of her time each day, because I wanted Marusia to excel in all her subjects so she wouldn't be sent to Kazakhstan, or Buriato-Mongolia and be able to continue with her studies. During the exams I helped her all I could. From my countryman who had contacts in the Gorono[24] and the directors of the technical school, I got the essay topics, I wrote the essays for her and left them for her to rewrite and submit at the exam.

One evening I found Marusia in a sad mood: our attempts at obtaining excellent marks in all her subjects had been in vain. The two best and most active representatives of the Communist Youth

---

[24] Russian abbreviation of *Gorodskoi otdel narodnogo obrazovaniia*, i.e., National Education Department, City Branch.

League were to be sent to the pedagogical institute. Only one of them had any proper knowledge of the work, the other knew nothing at all, even though his report showed excellent marks.

The other students were left to choose from Yakutia, Buriato-Mongolia, Komi-Zirian Republic, and the Sokhachovka region of Kursk Region. Neither Marusia nor I thought it suspicious that Sokhachovka lay on the same parallel as the Transarctic and the Transbaikal.

"If I wasn't lucky enough to get into the institute then at least I'll go west to teach, rather than east," Marusia said. "What do you think?"

I agreed with her wholeheartedly.

The day the young teachers received their postings the school was filled with lament and crying. The girls were lamenting their youth, which would waste away in the depths of Yakutia. Few believed in the possibility of continuing their education later on, or even returning home. One of the Communist Youth League gods appointed acting education officer for the town of Yakutsk went about with his nose up in the air and looked at everyone with contempt. The boys, looking more like *shpana* from the rag market than future teachers, were conferring in half-tones whether it was better to throw everything in and seek another profession or to go to the Transbaikal, get their papers there and then escape home. Little did they know that they would not receive their educational certificates there either.

Marusia was posted to Sokhachovka.

A few other girls with the same posting wept with everyone, though perhaps more loudly and sorrowfully than the rest. But neither Marusia nor I took much notice: we were hurrying off to the cinema, I think, and were not in the mood for weeping.

The next day I visited my countryman.

"Why didn't you come yesterday?" he lashed out at me. "There's a secret directive that five of the students are to remain in this town. Tell Marusia to see the director, they may just let her stay. Otherwise they'll send her off to the Buriats or, God forbid, to Sokhachovka..."

"Why do you say: God forbid, to Sokhachovka? That's just where she's been posted."

94

"Where?"

"Sokhachovka."

"And you two agreed? Does she or you, do any of you know what Sokhachovka is?"

"It's probably a large village or a small town. In any case I think it's better than the wilds of Komi-Ziriansk."

"You think! You should know, not think. Sokhachovka is a region of total syphilis."

In my nineteen years I had heard several words which kill. They seemed to me later, for I had not let them kill me, like the metallic glint of a knife poised over me. Petro Matviyovych's words were like a snake which had wrapped itself around me: other than the fear of death, the truth about Sokhachovka had in it an unspeakable, poisonous horror. I had experienced the terror of death many a time; it had become almost something normal. But the feeling which Sokhachovka evoked was new, unknown, encountered for the first time. I don't know why, but then as now I thought that the business involved more than just the life of a person.

She was still a child. She didn't know what syphilis was, and thought it to be some brutal Russian curse.

Our attempts at saving her did not meet with success. In vain she went to the director, in vain my countryman pleaded on her behalf. The lists were confirmed and nothing could be done.

The implacable hand of the law was evicting Marusia from her modest room in a quiet street and throwing her under the wheels of a new life. It evicted her so that she could be broken, corrupted, mixed with the others and made to be like them. I was sorry for this girl who had entered my life so unusually, bringing bright sunshine into the grey circle of my existence.

In the evenings I urged her to throw it all in and find a job as a cashier, a secretary, or a typist. She made no reply and only wept. I tried to placate her as best as I could. I still remember the salty taste of her tears on my lips.

Then I had to leave. I wrote to Marusia several times, but there was no reply; probably because I never stayed long enough in one place.

… And now we had finally met…

I walked along the snow-covered road which was being buried deeper and deeper by the snowstorm and from which I finally strayed. I faced the prospect of spending the night in the fields, the possibility of freezing to death, falling into a hole, being torn apart by wolves or going into a village and chancing on Soviet partisans or Germans. The Germans would have most certainly led me away to a hungry death in a concentration camp. The partisans, on the other hand, after my recent escape (I should have taken my passport with me!), would have executed me immediately. But I kept going. For what was captivity or death in comparison to the horror of horrors which I had left behind?

Sokhachovka lay behind me.

A JOKE

1

I dreamt that two giant dogs were barking and attacking me.
Their owner raced out of the house to defend me. He had a stick in
his hand; he raised his stick high and hit me over the shoulders
instead of hitting the dogs. After the blows there was nothing left
for me to do but to wake up.

It is said that if you have bad dreams, something good will
happen in reality. But this time dream and reality were as one. Only
instead of dogs I saw two enormous Germans, the taller one
holding a stick. The owner of the house wasn't even thinking of
defending me: he was the epitomy of confusion and fear, and I was
the last person on his mind. What I had taken for barking, was the
Germans saying:

"*Auf! Auf!*"

However I was allowed to put my boots on, and they didn't take
any notice of the fact that I was putting on new Soviet-made
officer's boots. The boots and the absence of any documents did
not prophesy anything good for me. My thoughts spun round like
a compass needle and stopped at one alternative: I had to make
tracks.

But the situation did not allow me to carry out my plan, neither
in the house, nor in the street where I was led out together with the
owner.

The Germans, as they had done several months before when I
had been taken prisoner, were ordering all the men out of the
houses and forming them into a long column. No one asked for
documents. Would I end up behind barbed wire again? But that
time it had been on the second day after the battle for the city, on
the front line; here we were deep in the rear, the front had passed
ages ago and the Red partisans from the neighbouring region had
not yet mounted any raids.

'No, they're probably taking us away to work. But all the same
I must escape,' I thought, glancing down at the toes of my boots
which were camouflaged by trouser legs, and wondering why the

guards did not notice such criminal things as new boots on me or anyone else.

When there were forty or more of us – the Soviets had cleaned the area out well so that only forty men, for the most part grandfathers and teenagers, remained in the whole village – we were ordered to set off. However, there were no avenues of escape: wide pastures under snow, houses no closer than fifty metres, guards at the front, back, and sides. And strange, unfamiliar villagers about me. I kept looking at the guards. All were handsome, tall, in mottled jackets and pants, in felt boots trimmed with leather, and with two zig-zags of white lightning on their collars.

As we moved along I deliberated why we were being taken, choosing from several possibilities. Perhaps the Soviet partisans had made their way into these parts and had caused trouble, and we were being taken hostage. Or we were required for some work project. Or even, this was possible too, a camp of prisoners had died or frozen out, and we were being taken to replenish the camp and were being made replacement POWs or *Ersatzkriegsgefangene.*

I tried to console myself with the fact that we were being taken west, where several dozen kilometres away Chernihiv[25] Region began, so that our column's itinerary coincided with my own plans. Outside the village a tank was standing at a road intersection. Several Germans were waiting for us. A smiling officer stepped forward. He obviously wanted to speak to us: the column stopped.

"Good-day, boys!" the officer called out in a cheerful resounding voice.

"*Zdrass!*" several voices answered in military fashion.

"Zdraviya zhelayu![26]" some old fellow blurted out.

Again I was convinced that when one anticipates the future and thinks about all the possible alternatives, then in reality one will be faced with an unconsidered or unexpected outcome.

The tank officer said something to the officer who had brought us here. A command rang out and the soldiers moved away,

---

[25] A northern region in Ukraine bordering Russia.
[26] "I wish you good health!" (Old Russian form of greeting)

standing in a crowd some distance away, their faces displaying nothing. Besides, I can't read German faces: try to understand a letter written in gothic script by an unknown author.

The officer addressed us: "At ease!"

We did. He told us with great joy that the German high command had decided to call on every man in the liberated territories capable of bearing arms to fight against a common enemy – Bolshevism. The peoples of Russia had to fight for their just place in a New Europe.

I watched him and thought: 'Is he telling the truth or poking fun at us?' It was only the winter of 1942: nothing had yet been heard about volunteers, and I had only come across a few Russian drivers in the columns of German transports. So I watched the speaker to see if his real thoughts would be betrayed by some facial expression and listened to his voice for hints of derision. His face was civil, handsome, happy, his voice clear and joyous, of a pleasing timbre, without the slightest German accent. Just that.

All of us, the officer said, would join the SS Division 'Viking'. In the nearest town we would be issued with uniforms and weapons, and sent to the front. Though I knew then that there was no absurdity the Germans wouldn't try in wartime, I still did not believe his words.

The speaker finished:

"Any questions?"

Someone responded from the rear:

"I'm a lame man. Do you understand, I'm lame. How can I join the army?"

"It's all right. We'll put you in an aeroplane. You won't need to walk."

This was an absolute farce. I grew terrified. My heart ached with impending tragedy.

"I'm sixty-six. Can I be expected to fight at my age?"

"Don't worry, there's a whole regiment of people like you, veterans of the First World War. You should see them fight! Any more questions?"

"May I relieve myself?" one of the boys burst out, beating me by half a second. I had wanted to ask the same question. It was the only way to gain thirty odd metres to escape.

99

"Hold on a while, impatient..." and the officer swore coarsely. There was less room left for doubt. Something had to happen.

Would we be taken to a prisoner-of-war camp? Shot? Or run over by a tank?

"No more questions?!" the officer ordered rather than asked, and suddenly gave the command: "Platoon, attention!"

We stood at attention and held our breath. The drill began: 'Eyes right! Quick march! Double time! Right shoulder fo'ward!' Again I heard the terminology of the Soviet Army, with which I had become acquainted while in the home guard.

This lasted fifteen to twenty minutes. The Germans on the highway roared with laughter seeing us bumbling about, trampling the snow. The old men, probably once tsarist soldiers, marched solemnly, those who had never been in the army fell out of step, and the cripple hobbled along. The guffaws and this idiotic drill left no doubt that we were being ridiculed, derided, and that in actual fact no one wanted to make us into a volunteer army.

We were moving in open line formation from the road toward a gully. I was second last in the left flank. We had treaded the snow firm by the roadside, but here it was fresh and the going was harder. However our rhythmic movements made it easier.

Funny, people are herded together, told to stand in lines, issued orders, and every one of them loses his individuality, becomes a mechanical part of some whole, succumbing to the powerful rhythmic force of military marching. Even an ardent individualist and anarchist like myself, who had never inwardly succumbed to anyone's power and as a rule felt, thought, and occasionally even acted as I myself felt fit, even I was partially overcome, subdued. I felt bound to these strange villagers with whom I was marching. Had the mathematician from the prisoner-of-war camp been right, when he denied individualism as such and proclaimed the automatism of man?

I looked ahead to the gully from where the tops of trees could be seen. I should make a run for it before it was too late. But would I have the courage? Had anyone anywhere the resolve and the strength to leave his detachment while 'on the march'? But I didn't have to be like everyone else. I had enough...

100

"Lie down!" The command sounded hard and sharp. I lay down in the snow with the rest. This after thoughts of escape! The officer's command had sounded before I had ordered myself to make a run for it. I obeyed the first command.

The others were lying prostrate, probably seeing no more than the snow before their faces. I had raised my head a little and turned it slightly to the right. I saw the officer followed by two soldiers leave the road and approach the right flank.

A thought flashed through my mind: 'They'll be removing our boots', and my toes grew numb with fright. How would I cover my bare feet? Would they let me cover them?

But they weren't interested in boots. The officer drew out a pistol, bent over the first man and fired twice into the back of his head. The body shuddered, stretched out and grew still. One of the villagers nearby stood up.

"Stay down!" the murderer whooped and bent over the second man. Again two shots.

All were lying motionless, as if they couldn't hear anything, as if they didn't know or understand what was happening. And I was lying in one row with them, my head slightly turned, and looking, my eyes turning out of their sockets. He bent over a third man, a fourth... Thirty-seven to thirty-eight men and fifty paces separated him from me. A solitary shot rang out: he'd run out of shells. The officer got another magazine. Two soldiers several steps behind him again slung their rifles across their shoulders. They were not needed. Their chief would finish everything himself.

A minute of deathly silence. I tensed my muscles, like an animal preparing to pounce, filled my lungs with air and suddenly like the crack of a rifle, only louder, an authoritative scream rang out:

"Company, double quick march!"

I jumped up and sped off straight for the gully, others tore off with me and behind me. Could anyone have thought that the order was given by a stray youth in a *kufayka* and officer's boots lying second-last in the left flank?

Shots crackled behind us. The bullets sang thinly and savagely. Someone fell in the snow right in front of me. Had he tripped, or was he dead? I bounded over him and continued running.

101

Then the heavy machine-gun from the tank responded. I found myself jumping from tree to tree, descending into the gully and tailing the others. Then the dense brambles tore at my face and clothes. There were only four of us left and we were clambering up the other side after following the gully around for a while. We were being chased by several German soldiers who occasionally fired short bursts from their machine-guns. Because I was running last, they were aiming specifically at me, unless it was just my imagination.

Then there were no more Germans, I had no longer had my hat, and we were walking through scrub toward the forest.

At last we stopped. Two youngsters, a bearded fellow, and me. Covered in hoar-frost, the tree's branches were entwined in fanciful silvery patterns against the azure sky. One of the boys was crying – his father hadn't made it to the gully. The other was silent and looked around with cow-like eyes. What were my eyes like then? I tied a handkerchief around my head so it wouldn't freeze too much. Wiping the blood from his scratched cheek, the bearded fellow asked me:

"Eh, squirt, do you know who gave the order to run? Because it wasn't the officer's voice and the order came from the left flank?"

I shrugged my shoulders without saying a word. For if I, frightened, teeth chattering, and trembling all over, had said it was me, he would never have believed me.

The bearded fellow scrutinised me, and receiving no answer, added:

"Your *kufayka*'s been shot through, brother..."

NIGHT WITH A NAKED GIRL

1

An idyllic inviolable icy silence dominated the settlement near the railway station.

The figures appeared two-dimensional, drawn sharply in black ink against the pink background of a fading sunset.

There were four figures. The number made me uneasy and I turned into the nearest side street: four seems to have something unfinished about it, demanding completion and... what if someone should decide to make me the fifth figure? This bade me no good, for the four coal-black figures were nothing other than the bodies of hanged men.

The side street was quite pleasant, with low latticed fences, orchards dusty with frost, and white three-windowed cottages.

A bareheaded solid woman of about forty stood smoking on the first porch, her hair permed, face thickly powdered and lips liberally smeared. The paint on her lips was applied in the form of a 'bow', so that the corners of her mouth were left unpainted. It looked as if she'd had a decent stiff drink and had stepped outside for a breath of fresh air.

I have a natural antipathy toward women wearing make-up and so I walked past the woman without asking her if I could have dinner there and stay the night.

And just as well, for in the neighbouring house I found sincere people and a delicious dinner.

White walls, curtains, a four-poster bed – all attested to domestic comfort and middle class prosperity. Odd volumes of Granat's encyclopedia, Alfred Brem, the 'Kobzar'[27], and several other books together represented all of mankind's culture.

In conversation I learned that the four I had assumed to be hanged were really only tied up. The Hungarians posted at the

---

[27] Granat's encyclopedia – the first multi-volume Russian encyclopedia produced by brothers Aleksandr and Ignatiy Granat; Alfred Brehm (1829-1884) was a German zoologist; 'Kobzar' – a popular book of poetry by Taras Shevchenko (1814-1861).

station strung their Jews up for all kinds of transgressions. They strung them up for two to three hours, then took them down.

They talked as friends would, sympathising with me.

True, they didn't let me sleep the night in the house, and escorted me to their 'dacha', as they called it. A spotted dog met us in the yard, politely wagging its tail. The man kicked away the iron bar which held the door closed and led me into a stall.

"The Hungarians tore off the lock," he explained. "They wanted to take the cow. So now the shed's unlocked."

In the glow of the man's cigarette lighter I first saw the cow, then sheaves of reeds, and beyond them a door in the wall leading to other quarters. It turned out to be a narrow, tidy room with a concrete floor, containing a vat, a millstone, gardening tools, a shuttered window, and most importantly of all a trestle-bed covered with a hay-mattress.

An old sheepskin coat torn at the flap and missing a left sleeve was to be my blanket.

When the owner left I searched by the light of matches, which were damp and hard to ignite, for a bolt or latch with which I could lock myself in the 'dacha', but discovered that there were no locks, only a hook which was fastened from inside the stall where the cow stood.

I groped my way to the bed, took off my quilted jacket and boots, wrapped my feet in the jacket, covered myself with the sheepskin coat and was fast asleep in two minutes.

I don't think I slept for long.

Impending danger woke me and threw me from the trestle-bed before I was aware of it.

Dogs barked and grew silent. I heard someone's light steps pass beside the 'dacha', there was a rustle, a click, a rattle, and the door to the stall creaked. Obviously someone well acquainted with the place was trying to make their way toward the door of my room in the darkness.

Barefoot, I hurried forward but tripped and brought something crashing to the ground the moment the door opened.

"Oh, who's here?" came a scream from the door.

It was a female voice.

104

"Don't be afraid, come in. But be careful, I've knocked some damn thing over."

"You're not Hungarian, are you?"

"Why should I be Hungarian?"

She whispered cautiously and entreatingly:

"Don't talk loudly, they're after me."

"Come inside. I'll lock the door." I wanted to strike a light but neither of the two remaining matches ignited. "Have you any matches?"

"I've nothing on me. Only a pair of galoshes and a scarf."

It was a starry, moonless night. The only thing by which I could orientate myself in this unfamiliar, cluttered room was a crack of light coming through the shutters.

My unknown visitor pushed past me.

"Careful! Don't fall. I've knocked something over."

I half closed the door and felt for the hook. The advantage of a hook over all locks, bolts, and latches is that it can be closed from both sides of the door. With a knife and enough time it can usually be unlocked from the other side too.

I raised the hook and set it so that it would fall at the slightest jolt. With a fast jerk, so as to make a minimum of noise, I tapped the door once – the hook was far too high and refused to fall, I tapped a second time and it fell much too early, but the third time the door locked.

Just like in a fairy-tale: the first arrow falls short, the second overshoots its mark, and the third goes straight into the heart.

"Don't make so much noise, they'll hear you. They're looking for me. Hear the dogs barking?" a muffled whisper came from behind.

"There was a pitchfork here," I said, and moved my hand to where, according to my calculations, the gardening tools should have been.

Instead of the pitchfork my hand touched something cold and elastic.

"It's me," came a whisper from the darkness. "Where are you putting your hand!"

"You're completely naked? You must be cold ..." Only now did her words about the scarf and the galoshes register.

"I was bathing when they broke in... "

"There's a sheepskin on the bed, put it on."

"Sh!" she grabbed my arm. "They're in the yard, knocking at the owner's house. Listen! And I didn't even lock the stall. They'll discover the two of us... "

"Don't get upset. There are many things far worse than death." I took a step toward her and put my arm around her scarf-covered shoulder. My foot caught something. I bent down — it was a handle; running my fingers over it I discovered it was the pitchfork which I was looking for and which I had knocked over while rising to meet my nocturnal visitor.

I lifted the pitchfork silently, thank heavens. Just in time too. The outside door creaked and the stall filled with the voices of several men.

I clutched the pitchfork with both hands and we stood stock still.

The light of an electric torch ran over the door and two white streaks fell on us, the third fell to one side. For a moment I saw her knee, and my hand holding the pitchfork.

We felt we were already discovered, that we could already be seen. But the cracks in the door were far too small for them to notice us.

I thought I caught the smell of vodka. Maybe it was the soldiers on the other side of the door. Or perhaps it was just my imagination.

Close by I heard the words of a language unknown to me. Then the rustle of straw, the violent rattling of the closed door and the icy squeak of receding footsteps.

We stood motionless for a while.

I felt the warmth of her breath near my left ear.

"They've gone ..." she said, sounding disconcerted. "They were so close, right at the door, and didn't find us... Unbelievable."

"We were saved by the hook. I fastened the hook on the other side of the door and they thought there was no one here."

"The hook's on the other side?"

"Yes. And now we can't leave here until someone lets us out."

"Auntie stayed behind," the visitor said without any connection to the subject of our discussion. "I escaped, but she wasn't fast enough."

2

Her teeth began to chatter. Mine too. Several minutes of standing barefoot on a cold floor were having their effect. I found the sheepskin coat and the quilted jacket and gave them to her. But that didn't make me any warmer. By huddling together we could have both kept warm. But who knew if the Hungarian soldier in me would not be aroused?

Having made herself comfortable on the bed, she proceeded to tell me about herself in a voice hoarse from either fright or cold. I learnt her name was Alia, that she was seventeen, that she had finished ninth grade and was living with her aunt.

"Siegfried and Brunhilde," I said after a minute's silence, "lay a sword between them when they slept side by side. Perhaps we could do the same, by placing the pitchfork between us?"

From her silence I realised that she knew nothing about Siegfried. My remark had created a certain falseness. I felt this and tried to justify myself.

"Siegfried is a hero in ancient Germanic poetry. Do you like poetry?"

"Yes, especially Mayakovsky... 'A Cloud in Trousers', 'Seated', 'My Soviet Passport'..."

The name Mayakovsky stirs up a physical disgust within me, and I said:

"Br-r, what filth."

"Why filth?" she was offended. "Even," she lowered her voice, "comrade Stalin himself said: 'Mayakovsky was and remains the best and most talented poet of our socialist era, and to show indifference toward his memory and his work is a crime.'"

"You still remember what Stalin said? He wrote on one of Gorky's early works: 'This piece is stronger than Goethe's 'Faust'...' Caucasian mules understand nothing in the field of poetry."

107

"So you're one of those!" she moved away. The Soviet government educated you, and you..."

"Oh, yes," I interjected. "Obviously caring about my education, the Soviets signed me up several times for 'the highest measure of social education – execution'." I had used the words 'social education' instead of 'social protection' on purpose.

"Pity they didn't execute you."

"Great! And who would have rescued you then from the Hungarian rapists?"

"You rescued me? If it wasn't for you and traitors and cowards like you, no enemy would have crossed the sacred borders of our socialist fatherland. But now, because of people like you, the dirty boots of German fascists and their henchmen are trampling our soil."

...So this was whom I had hidden... This was whom I was ready to shield from bullets and bayonets with my chest...

"Listen... I'd urge you to check your propagandist fervour. I've heard enough of this garbage. And my fatherland, in case you want to know, is quite different to yours. Now, if you'll let me have my jacket back, I'd like to go to sleep. If you're afraid of freezing, lay down beside me. I'm not a Hungarian, and you don't exist for me as a woman."

I woke up late. On top of the quilted jacket was a sheepskin coat. My night visitor was no longer beside me. She couldn't have let herself out, so someone must have unlatched the hook. What a pity, I hadn't even seen her face.

I was putting my shoes on when the owner entered the 'dacha'.

"Ah, getting up. Well, get up and come have breakfast. Well," he winked roguishly, "how did you sleep?"

"Like Alfred Brehm – in one bed with a lioness..."

We entered the house.

"Tell me about it, before the wife comes."

I told him.

"All lies," the owner replied.

I looked at him in disbelief, thinking he had taken my story for an invention.

"She's as much her aunt, as I'm your uncle. And her name's Niurka, not Alia, and she was seventeen ages ago... Hear her voice? Too much alcohol or whatever. She knew you were sleeping in our 'dacha' because this same 'aunt' of hers saw you come into our place."

I interrupted him:

"Was that her on the neighbour's porch, all made up, smoking a cigarette?"

"Of course it was her. You wouldn't find another shaggy witch like her for a hundred miles around. While the Germans were stationed here they lived it up with them, now they're fooling round with the Hungarians. Damned activists."

"Then why did she..."

"Because usually two or three come to visit them, but yesterday a whole crowd came round. Niurochka must have upped in what she had on and dashed off to you. And you lost your head."

THE GOLDEN CELLAR

1

And then I remembered another meeting with another girl.

The circumstances of this meeting were much the same as those leading to the encounter of the day before. I had left the road because that time I had been faced with real danger.

It happened shortly after my leaving the town of N., toward the end of a short winter's day. On the side of the highway along which I was walking I noticed a dead body clothed in grey rags. I paid no attention to this. But half a kilometre further on I noticed two more bodies and pools of blood near them. Then there were more corpses, both with and without bloodstains, one, three, seven — I forget how many. Their faces were soil-grey, the clothes were remnants of Soviet military uniforms: prisoners had passed this way.

Later, beyond the woods, I saw the prisoners themselves camped in a valley on a road leading to the village that I was trying to reach. I would have to pass through their camp. This seemed rather dangerous. Although I had a passport and a pass with a skilfully forged stamp, the passport still bore signs of the old lettering, and its contents did not answer my description. The pass was written by hand in such suspect German, that I dared only show it to the village chairman or to the police[28]. My mind was still fresh with memories of guards grabbing chance passers-by to replenish our column, asking no questions about documents.

So I turned off the highway into the forest, making a detour to enter the village by another road.

But wandering through snow-drifts is no easy matter. A seemingly short distance stretches to infinity in snow, and by nightfall, having covered less than a third of the way, I emerged in a sheltered clearing where I could see two haystacks. I figured that rather than scramble through the snow and then be forced to knock on doors late at night, it would be better to spend the night in the hay.

---

[28] Policemen in villages were recruited from the local population.

It was completely light when the cold drove me from my den. I brushed the straw off and jogged around the stack to exercise my stiff legs. I raced around the corner and stopped: beside the other stack a dark figure was bending over. Someone was washing with snow.

I wanted neither meetings nor conversations with strangers, nor journeys with accidental companions. I was already looking forward to a solitary trek through the forest, and here was the possibility of unnecessary talk with an undesired stranger.

I wanted to retreat, but the figure straightened and looked in my direction.

Now my retreat could be taken for escape... So instead of returning behind the stack, I proceeded toward the person who no longer looked in my direction, but continued washing, as if ignoring me. I regretted not having turned back.

"Good morning, countryman!" I called out from afar.

"Good morning, countrywoman!" the figure replied, straightening again.

Thick chestnut-brown hair cascaded onto a fur collar, the face was red from the snow, the voice youthful and fresh. A girl!

I stopped in my tracks, so unexpected was the discovery, and looked over the half-covered piles of hay at the base of the stack, seeking a possible companion. But I saw no one. Though it seemed quite improbable, she was evidently alone.

"Come closer, don't be afraid!" she added in a slightly mocking voice, noting my confusion.

"Actually, I don't know which of us should be more afraid," I smiled as I approached. "I'm sorry, I took you for a man, and you're a woman." I looked at her quilted trousers and wanted to add something but desisted.

She smiled back haughtily:

"Firstly, a girl, not a woman, and secondly, careful with your sentences! As for me, I still haven't worked out," she added suddenly, "whether you're a man or an old woman."

Only then I remembered that I had tied my jaw with a handkerchief the size of a bed sheet, afraid my teeth might freeze.

"*Verflucht!*" I swore and quickly removed the handkerchief. "As far back as I can remember I've always been a man."

"Doesn't much look it... But let's suppose..."

"Oh, I see you're a real heroine. You're not only unafraid to spend the night on your own in the forest, but..."

"Who am I supposed to fear? You? Then step closer!"

Was this a challenge, or an invitation? I went up to her.

"Maybe you want to test your strength on me?"

"Why not?" And in jest I attempted to embrace her.

That moment, with an unexpectedly agile movement she brought my hat over my eyes, hit me under the breastbone, tripped me, and there I was lying supine on the hay.

It took me a tenth of a second to shift the hat from my eyes, and she needed just that much time to cover me with an armful of straw.

"Maybe she's a crim?' I thought, throwing the straw aside with both hands and crawled out. Without thinking further I blurted out the password[29].

But the three magic words which lowered raised revolvers, stayed the descent of knives, stopped hands ready to punch — these words made no impression on her.

"What?" she asked, standing warily before me.

Had she taken my joke for an attack?

"I said: 'Fair weather day'."

This was a widely used formula if one couldn't or didn't want to repeat a sentence not understood by someone. But on this day the phrase corresponded to reality: the day really promised to be a fine one. A light frost, no wind, clear, almost ringing air, two parallel tender pinkish-gold stripes of cloud on the horizon and a ray of morning sunshine from behind the stack lit up her face, reflected off her red jumper, and made the complexion of her forehead and cheeks appear pale pink and her lips cherry red.

Dark chestnut-brown hair, eyes unexpectedly blue, only not the colour of the sky which was far too pale now, but darker and sterner...

Suddenly she saw my face elongate, my eyes become round as saucers and my jaw drop.

---

[29] The underworld password was '*Porvy, porvy rubashku*' (Tear, tear the shirt). There was also a password for minor incidents: '*Po adresu?*' (Do you have the right place?) – author's footnote.

"What can it be?" I asked, looking past her into the forest depths.

She glanced around. In the same instant I swiftly gathered her up and threw her into the pile of straw and snow.

Actually, this was the only method I had read about in crime novels which could be put to practical use and I had once fallen victim to its effectiveness.

Before she could get up I offered her my hand, smiling:

"Come on, up you get."

She stood up and still holding my hand, said:

"Let's introduce ourselves. I'm Nina."

I told her my name, and drew back: I had told her my real name under which I had been convicted in 1930 and which I had not revealed to anyone since, not even to the friend I had risked my life for, not even to the other one who had risked his life for me.

"What's the matter?"

"Nothing. Just that in your presence I'm beginning to lose my self-control. I've told you my real name. It's the first time in ten years that such a thing has happened to me."

She laughed. Then noticing the snow on her clothes, remarked:

"It's not fair on your part: I threw you onto the straw but you threw me into snow. Help me brush it off."

We brushed the snow and straw from each other's clothes. Then I brought out my bag and we had breakfast. Her rations were just as meagre as mine.

For a while we would be travelling in the same direction.

We set off together, laughing and playfully jostling each other.

The long shadows of the pines appeared blue on the white snow.

I tried to recite some poetry, but the poems did not come. Their impact seems to diminish the more open space there is around. The very words which agitate, delight and soothe the senses, bringing tears to one's eyes in a small room, will pale and become lost in a forest or field among the true poetry of nature, vanishing without making an impression on our senses.

"You know," she said, interrupting me in mid verse, "when you tried to grab me with your paws, I wanted to teach you a lesson."

"But it turned out that I was more learned and experienced than you."

"Not more, I think. Have you ever been in prison?"

"'He who has not sat in prison is not a man'."

"Well, have you ever awaited execution?"

"Exactly eleven years ago in the -y district prison." (I named the area I hailed from). "It was a long time ago, but it's the truth."

"Have you ever had to kill anyone?"

I grew disconcerted.

"How should I put it... I've been sent off on 'dirty business', and I took part in a manhunt, and legally I was an accomplice in several cases. But I can't say that I have directly killed someone with my own hand."

"You see..." she uttered triumphantly, as if wanting to confirm something, and then interrupted herself: "Do you know Mikhailov?"

"Mikhailov? The one who was chief of police in N. and then ran off to join the Bolsheviks? Of course I know him..."

"He didn't run off anywhere."

"What do you mean, he didn't run off anywhere? I know for a fact that he did. It was said that the Germans executed him, but that's not true. The deputy burgomaster himself told my..."

"He knows nothing, your deputy burgomaster. Do you want to hear how it happened? But don't doubt my words. Lies are weapons of the weak. I belong to the strong and have no need to lie."

2

"Well, I could begin like this...

"A greying old granny went out into the orchard to gather some apples and noticed someone hiding in the raspberry patch. 'Someone's probably come to steal my apples', the old woman thought. But the interloper did not run off. Without getting up he put his finger to his lips so the old woman would not create a commotion, and begged in a whisper:

"'Gran, fetch me a piece of bread. Even a crust will do...'

114

"The thief was wearing the uniform of a Soviet army lieutenant, but had no belt or shoulder strap, and on his feet he wore shoes without laces in place of boots.

"To cut a long story short, I was the lieutenant.

"This was one of the most critical moments in my life. Either she kicked up a fuss and I would be caught, or… But she invited me inside, fed me and began questioning me. I told her the truth: that I had slapped a major who had made advances toward me; that my action was regarded as a severe transgression of military discipline; that a doctor friend had confirmed that I was ill; and that I was sent to a military hospital to recuperate and would then be shot.

"And also that I had escaped from the hospital the night before and that I probably wouldn't be found unless someone turned me in.

"The old woman broke down after hearing my story. She then locked me in the house and went out. Five or ten minutes later she returned and, without a word, led me to the entrance hall, and thence into some small pantry, or *chulanchyk* as she called it. There she showed me a trapdoor covered with an old rug. Stairs led down into a cellar. The old granny groped around for a switch and turned the light on. We went down. What could there be inside a cellar? Potatoes, carrots, onions, an empty barrel, some boxes. The old woman asked me to shift one of the boxes, scraped away some dirt with a shovel, and I saw another trapdoor appear. We just managed to open it. It was massive, made of iron, and didn't open upwards, but slid to one side. A narrow ladder led down into darkness: there was yet another cellar under this one.

"'You'll stay here until the Germans come. There are some boards down there you can sit on. Careful you don't bang your head. My husband will be back from work shortly; he'll bring you a mattress and dinner. Ah, I almost forgot, here's a candle and some matches.'

"I thought then that this woman must have lived through a lot in her lifetime to be able to save strangers so simply and naturally.

"I climbed down, the trapdoor slowly closed above me. After lighting a match I saw heavy stone walls, a ladder, boards placed on two saw-horses, mouldy brick walls. . .

115

"In the evening, although I didn't know what time it was, of course, the granny's husband came. He was twelve, perhaps even fifteen years her junior. Later I became convinced that they were ideally matched. Have you noticed that harmonious marriages most often occur where the woman is much older than the man? Maybe then there is something motherly in her attitude toward the man?"

Unlike many people, I can listen to other people's stories without interrupting, but seeing as she had put a question to me, I had to reply:

"The opposite happens too, when the man is twice the woman's age and virtually becomes her psychological father. Take for example Edgar Allan Poe and his 'Annabel Lee'. But then this phenomenon is rare, since it is well known that women have a preference for..."

"All right, then, 'they have a preference for...' Listen further. He brought me a mattress and dinner. I told him my adventures too. He told me his name was Abram Borisovich Peretz, and his wife's was Solomonia Markivna, and that he'd tell me about himself when the Germans came. Until then I could live in the cellar and feel at home.

"And so my life with the Peretzes began.

"During air raids they came down with me and stayed for several hours until everything quietened down. They enjoyed being with me and talking. During the bombing they prayed and taught me to pray. Before this I had known only 'Our Father', and only half of that. They also brought me a bible.

"At first I tried to read by the light of the candle, but soon gave up because there wasn't enough air. Though the vault had a narrow opening and air entered through a vent in the foundations and then into the cellar, it was nowhere near enough.

"Sometimes I went out at night to breathe the fresh open air and look at the stars. But this was dangerous. Women from the 'street committee' were on duty and militiamen roamed the streets. Then it became more dangerous to come out at night than in the day: the round-up of deserters had begun.

"And then my torture began.

"Uncle Abram brought another 'lodger' into my cellar, his most sincere adherent and best friend, as he said. But I disliked his

116

'adherent' at first glance. He was a man of thirty-two or thirty-three, olive-skinned, with deep wrinkles on his face. He was the stereotype model Soviet citizen. He wouldn't let Uncle Abram introduce us, saying 'it would be better for her not to know who I am, and vice versa.' After Uncle Abram climbed out and slid the trapdoor shut, he began carrying on about how pleasantly impressed he was that he would not be alone, but in company… well, and so on, everything people usually say on such occasions. I sat huddled up in a corner, watching him by the light of the candle, and thinking that I, on the contrary, derived no pleasure from his presence.

"Then he began excusing himself for not revealing his name: he couldn't because of certain considerations. But so that we could somehow address each other, he asked me to call him Max, and he'd call me Lucia, because Lucia is a name you can derive from every female name: Alexandra — Lucia, Olga — Lucia, Liudmila — Lucia. 'Every snotty country Akulka who arrives in the city becomes Lucia'.

"I stopped him, saying he was no Max to me, but a stranger, and if he liked, I'd call him Maxim Ivanovych[30]. And also that my name was Nina and I didn't keep it a secret. He probably didn't like being transformed from a romantic Max to an ordinary Maxim. In that case, he said, he wasn't Maxim, but Maximillian.

"You might ask why I didn't go back home. I tried earlier, before Maximillian's appearance, but nothing came of it. I couldn't go in my uniform, and Solomonia Markivna was only shoulder high to me and her clothes wouldn't fit."

As she paused in the recounting of her experience, I looked my companion up and down: she was my height exactly. For a woman, that's tall.

"I needed to get clothing and the Peretzes were afraid of rousing suspicion. They bought a few things for me at the flea-market, the rest Solomonia Markivna sewed herself. She sewed slowly, for the running of the house rested on her shoulders. Because it was wartime, city people bought everything being offered for sale,

---

[30] The formal way of addressing someone – by given name and patronymic.

whether they needed it or not, and waiting in queues was time-consuming.

"So a month passed before I was dressed and shod.

"But I had no luck with my journey.

"The Peretzes continually tried to dissuade me from leaving, saying the Germans would be here any day now, that going without papers was madness because they were hunting spies everywhere, and even if I reached home, it was the most dangerous place to hide.

"I told them it wasn't far away, that I'd get there in three days, and now that anarchy prevailed no one would look for me at home.

"Finally they blessed me, gave me food and money, and assured me that in case I should return, they would gladly have me back.

"But as I said, I had no luck. That first day I was detained by a collective farm brigade leader. The collective farmers surrounded me as if I were a wild beast. It was ugly and shameful..."

"And you had to lie your way out."

"And I had to lie my way out, but I lied too much and became confused. A militiaman arrived and took me into town. He led me slowly, unwillingly it seemed, then finally turned off the main road where I thought the militia station was and asked me in a side street if I had any money.

"I gave him the thirty roubles I had.

"He pocketed the money and said:

"'You can go now, citizen!'

"Even after this I didn't want to return to the Peretzes, and I wouldn't have returned there except for an old fellow I met who told me that the place I was going to was already under German control and that the front was only fifty kilometres away. I believed him, though as it turned out later, this was an utter lie. I still can't understand it. Why did he have to lie?"

She asked me the question and I replied:

"There are utilitarian liars who profit from lying, and there are people who, by inventing and embellishing an event, hope to impress others, or at least themselves. Obviously the old codger belonged to the second category, the aesthetic liars."

"Alright, but that's beside the point. So I returned to the Peretzes and again found myself in the secret cellar alone with my thoughts.

118

You know, people need such isolation for short periods. Thoughts emerge for which you just have no time because of everyday worries.

"I had a friend, his name was Vitaliy... Do you know what it is to have a real friend? I thought most about him. He was taken to the front straight out of fifth grade as an ordinary private..."

I admit that at the mention of Vitaliy an unpleasant feeling awoke within me. Was it jealousy perhaps?

She must have noticed the change in my expression, for she immediately changed the subject:

"I couldn't read: with the candle burning there was a shortage of air after half an hour.

"One night in the orchard I found a rotten stump that glowed with a phosphorescent light. I gathered some rotten pieces of wood and stood them in various corners of the cellar. They helped me orient myself and enabled me to move about more freely without the fear of breaking a leg or bashing my head in. The day Uncle Abram brought in his Maximillian, I could already differentiate objects by the light of these rotten logs.

"A little later Uncle Abram brought in a hurriedly-made straw mattress and stayed with us a while to chat. Solomonia Markivna came down with him, but Maximillian did all the talking.

"He said that these last few years he had lost faith in people. The economy had been rebuilt, life had been reorganised, and people were made into new beings, capable only of mechanical obedience. Ignatius Loyola had once wanted every member of the Jesuit Order to be in the order's hands like a corpse. But the new order had managed to make two hundred million behave like corpses in the hands of the Party. And only now had he realised that he was wrong. People's hearts had seemed as empty as the rooms of a deserted house. But now he believed that there were many who had found a secret corner in their hearts where they hid all their best traits. Soon, he said, the reign of terror would end and the eternal qualities of humanity would surface, as surely as we would leave this cellar.

"He knew about Loyola, so he wasn't a stereotype Soviet as I had at first thought. That was good. And what he said was true. However, he lacked sincerity.

"Have you noticed that the truth can be told without sincerity, and lies can be told sincerely?"

I had never thought about this problem and so I had no answer. Meanwhile, she continued.

"Applying your label, he was an 'aesthetic utilitarian'. He was a master of the spoken word and used his art toward some goal which I did not yet know. To place art in the service of a certain ambition is the basest, most underhanded thing a person can lower himself to. Isn't that right?"

"Yes," I said. "And when you meet a person who thinks exactly as you do, the feeling of isolation disappears. But please continue, I don't want to interrupt..."

"So when they left we sat a while with the candle burning. He talked, I was silent and ignored him. Then I interrupted him and said I was going to sleep, turned away and pretended to have fallen asleep. But sleep was the last thing on my mind. The presence of this 'well brought-up and noble man', to quote the Peretzes, bade me no good. When the candle burnt out I took the lieutenant's breeches from under my head and put them on for safety ... I should have armed myself with a stick, but there was nothing suitable nearby.

"I don't know how or when I fell asleep, but I woke when I felt someone's touch. This character who had just been talking garbage about gentlemanly conduct with women, was bent over me and was feeling my knees. Obviously my breeches had surprised and confused him. His hand moved away for a moment. This saved me.

"He didn't know two things: that I had finished the Lesgaft Institute[31], and that I could make him out in the light of the rotten logs.

"I rolled over onto my back and drew my legs in. When he bent over again I straightened out and let him have it with both feet in the midriff. Something cracked inside him and he flew into the emptiness. There was a crash and then silence. Had I killed him?

"No, I saw him get up, feel his way to his mattress and lie down.

"Not a word was said between us.

---

[31] Institute for Physical Education in Leningrad (now the Lesgaft National State University of Physical Education, Sport and Health, St. Petersburg).

"But the war between us had begun.

"Of course, I didn't sleep a wink that night. And the next day as soon as Abram Borisovich came down I announced that I was going home. But Abram Borisovich did not listen to me. He was preoccupied with his own troubles: he had been called up to appear 'with cup and spoon', probably to be sent to serve on the home front, or to be attached to the home guard being organised. So he had come down into the cellar to become its third occupant.

"Now I was safe: there would be no more attacks on my person.

"But imagine the pleasantness: two men and me!

"This lasted almost two weeks.

"One night the militia appeared, searched the rooms, the shed, and went into the upper cellar. The loft was locked so they ripped the trapdoor off its hinges without waiting for it to be opened. They were looking for the owner who had 'avoided mobilisation' and were very surprised to find no one.

"I remember the night the Germans shelled the city with mortars. All four of us were gathered in the cellar: Abram Borisovich, Solomonia Markivna, Maximillian, and me.

"We could hear the explosions coming closer and closer. The fear of the three frightened people infected me too. I confess, I was afraid.

"Choosing a moment when there was a lull in the shelling. Uncle Abram asked for our attention and began a solemn speech. First he told us about himself: he was once a merchant and an industrialist in Uman. The revolution caught him in Moscow, so he managed to stay alive. He had found his wife after the civil war and they moved here.

"He talked clumsily, continually repeating himself. Then he moved to the present day.

"It might happen, he said, that a bomb or bullet would kill them, and we younger ones would remain. So he had decided to reveal a secret to us, the heirs to his wealth, which was not in the rooms above, but which was here in the cellar. Here in this wall, so many paces from the corner, and so much up from the floor, there was buried a chest full of gold. They had been robbed, their house had been ransacked many a time back in Uman, and although their millions had perished, something had still remained. There were two hundred thousand roubles in bank notes and promisory notes, and thirty-five thousand in gold.

"All this time I was watching Maximillian (Uncle Abram called him Serhiy, by the way). I realised why he had conned his way into the cellar and what his fiery speeches were leading to: he had suspected or known about the gold, and it had attracted him.

"Should I tell the Peretzes about my hunch? No, it was too late, and besides they wouldn't have believed me. I had fallen from their grace enough, by acting far too coldly toward their darling friend. They obviously hoped we would make a couple. Solomonia Markivna had even whispered into my ear several times that he was far too discreet and irresolute and that I should woo him myself. I just looked at the savage expression on his face and kept quiet.

"Then the Germans came. We moved upstairs and Maximillian disappeared. Several days later, just when most men were being interned in camps, he reappeared again, this time as Serhiy Mikhailov, one of the leaders of the newly formed police force. How he had wormed his way into this position, who had recommended him, what connections he had, I still don't know.

"I spent two more weeks with the Peretzes, until I knew for certain that our town was occupied by the Germans too, and then I returned home.

"We had a Murillo[32] at home, a genuine, though small icon of the Holy Mother. And mother said (I've got a mother and a younger sister at home, father's passed away), well mother said: 'Take the Peretzes a gift from me.'

"It didn't take me long: I got ready and set out.

"... I reached their house just as they were being led away. From a block away I saw two soldiers leave the house escorting the old couple out, but I was too far away to comprehend what was happening. I almost ran, but before I had reached the Peretzes' place they had been put in a truck covered with canvas and driven away. An officer and a civilian in a beaver coat got into a private car and sped off.

---

[32] Bartolomé Esteban Murillo (1617-1682), a Spanish Baroque painter best known for his religious works.

122

"Some suspicious-looking men and women who had previously been hanging about the gates of neighbouring houses with looks of indifferent bystanders, rushed toward the empty house.

"An old fellow in felt boots ran past me.

"Two policemen came jogging around the corner with bands on their arms and carrying truncheons.

"'Back!' they shouted. 'These are the quarters of the new police chief!'

"Several old women who had managed to get inside were turfed out.

"I asked someone what had happened.

"'You don't know what's happened? They've taken the Jews away.'

"I gasped that the Peretzes weren't Jews.

"They know better up there, I was told.

"I ran to the commandant's office, from there I was sent to the gendarmerie, from there to the gestapo. The Peretzes' fate lay in the hands of the people here.

"I already knew about the Germans' exceptional venality and already dreamed of securing the Peretzes' release with my Murillo.

"I was received by a blond officer in the presence of an interpreter. I told him why I had come and assured him that I knew these people and could vouch with my life if they wanted it, that neither of them were Jewish.

"'Better not be so hasty,' the interpreter said to me. 'Do you know that people caught harbouring Jews are executed too?' And then he added more gently. Take even their names: Abram Peretz, Abram Borisovich – he's not Borisovich, but Borukhovich. And she is Solomonia Markivna. Maybe she's Salomea, the one who danced before Satan?'

"'But he's a Ukrainian from Uman,' I persisted.

"'Every Jew who hails from Ukraine is a 'Ukrainian', from Poland — a 'Pole'. There were Jews from Russia in Germany who called themselves 'Russians',' he went on.

"Then, like a drowning person clutching at straws, I seized on a last possibility in which I didn't believe myself.

"But Mr. Serhiy Mikhailov knows them well, he's in the police force. I think he will vouch for them too, I said.

"The interpreter told the chief this, the chief smiled and said something back to the interpreter. He smiled too and said nothing.

"But I can speak a little German and I knew what they were saying. That the Peretzes were taken following Mikhailov's denunciation.

"A long silence followed. I had forgotten the Murillo and everything else in the world. The interpreter probably gathered from my expression that I understood. I don't know what I would have said or how I would have acted, however several gestapo men entered the room and the interpreter asked me to leave.

"From there I went to the town council to confer with one of the officials who had visited the Peretzes while I was there. He was not in.

"In the street I realised to my horror that I no longer had the painting with me. Once more I did the rounds of the town council, the gestapo, the gendarmerie, and the command, but found no trace of my mislaid parcel.

"In the passage of the command headquarters I came across the man in the beaver coat. It was Mikhailov. Fortunately he didn't notice me or recognise me.

"I went to the home of the official who had visited the Peretzes. I was received with restraint, but nevertheless received. I spent the night with them. I say spent, because I didn't sleep that night.

"The next morning I went to the Peretzes' house and carefully tried their front door. It was locked. I circled the house and tried the back door. It was closed too.

"All was quiet and deserted. I removed my coat and took it into the toilet so no one would steal it.

"From the kitchen window I removed a sheet of cardboard which had replaced a pane of glass lost during the bombing. Then I put my hand in, opened the window and climbed into the kitchen. Taking my shoes off and trying to make as little noise as possible I explored the house.

"Had he really managed to come here yesterday, I thought? But I had seen him at command headquarters. No, he would still come,

124

I decided. Where should I wait for him? In the house or down there?

"Perhaps he was somewhere here now, I figured, for the police had said that this was now the police chief's residence.

"I thought I heard the echoes of muffled blows. I entered the *chulanchyk*. The trapdoor to the first cellar was closed, but the mat which hid it was lying to one side.

"I could hear the blows quite clearly now.

"There had been no electricity for some time and I groped my way down the stairs. The trapdoor to the lower cellar was open (it could be opened and closed only from the top). A soft rustling sound came from the cellar and I saw the glimmer of a light. . .

"I crawled up to the opening and looked in. On the boards where my mattress had once lain stood a 'flying-fox' lantern, its light illuminating a wall with a gaping black hole.

"A person bending over, whose face I could not see, was feverishly tearing at the wrapping of a small broken chest and throwing aside rolls of banknotes.

"I watched for a long time: on the boards beside the person lay his tools: a hammer, chisel, and pliers, a spade stood against the wall. Another small thing lay black beside the lantern, out of its light, but I couldn't work out what it was. But that was not important: the main thing was that he had no crowbar.

"The person crawled on all fours, wallowing in the money like a dog. Then he put his hand in the hole and pulled out what seemed like a tin can, opened it and brought a handful of something up to the light of the lantern to examine it. The light reeled with the dull glow of gold in his hand.

"'Mikhailov!' I said with extreme calm and not too loudly, but carefully enunciating every word. 'This gold is your death.'

"He jumped to his feet and grabbed the thing lying near the lantern which I could not make out.

"It was a revolver.

"Here, look..."

She unbuttoned her coat and eased it off one shoulder. On the very top of her red jumper was a spot patched with grey thread.

"That's from the bullet. A few centimetres lower and... but I slid the trapdoor shut before he could hit me."

She grew silent.

"And that's about it. I fitted a board into the trapdoor so that it couldn't be slid open without first removing the wood, covered everything with soil, stood a barrel of sauerkraut on top and covered the entry to the upper cellar with the mat, returning the way I had come.

"For almost two weeks after this I lived with the bureaucrats. They weren't too pleased about it, but I fed myself and gave them food too. I was waiting, hoping the Peretzes might be released.

"On the tenth day I learned that they were no longer alive."

Again she was silent. I looked at her face, her lips were trembling, tears glistened in her eyes.

"Well, here we are then," she said, and stopped.

"Where?"

"Can't you see? We're at the crossroads. You have to go west, I need to go south. I've been this way twice before, I should know."

An inexpressible gloom seemed to pervade her voice. Was it the effect of the story she had just told me?

"Well then. There's no chance of us ever meeting again, so it's goodbye!"

I shook her hand, and still holding it, asked:

"Tell me, Nina, if they really were Jews, would you have…"

"Avenged them? What do you think? Of course I would have."

Wordlessly I shook her hand.

"You see, I'm very sensitive to how people react to my words and actions," she said, "And while I was talking I felt that you experienced the same feelings as I did. And I'm convinced that I know you now no worse than you know me. Anyhow, we'll be standing here till nightfall like this. Goodbye."

She shook my hand firmly, like a man.

But our hands wouldn't part, as if they were tied together.

I moved half a step closer and caught her knee between mine, then transferred her right hand into my left and brought it behind my back, meanwhile trying to make her left hand harmless with my right. She threw her head back and closed her eyes. I seemed to forcibly reach her lips with mine and was surprised when she responded to my kiss.

Suddenly she pushed me away and freed herself from my embrace.

Our eyes met again. She placed her hand on my shoulder and kissed me quickly and resolutely. "Go now. Our paths are parting."

"Nina!" I yelled after her. "Nina, there's another small thing."

She stopped, I drew closer:

"If ever you're in danger then don't forget this phrase..." I repeated the words I had said to her that morning.

"What is it? Some password? Are you an *urka*?"

"No, just a student. But I've lived with thieves."

"All right then, don't come any closer. Goodbye."

She waved to me, turned around and quickly walked off.

Why hadn't I run after her then and gone with her?

HOME

1

I wasn't at all surprised that I had failed to see the crosses on the village church, or the church itself with its high bell tower as I approached my village. After all, I hadn't seen any churches while I was on the road. I was surprised and slightly uneasy about not being able to recognise the surroundings. From where I was coming the village should have been almost completely hidden by a stand of trees, to the right of the trees should have been a solitary farmstead surrounded by a ditch bordered with poplars, and to the left there should have been a communal storehouse, officially called a *magazin*, but which all the villagers steadfastly called a *hamazin* or *hamazai*. There was none of this. Neither the trees, nor the pointed poplars, nor the grey *hamazai*.

A straight wide road bordered by ditches and quite foreign to me brought me to the first houses of an unknown street. This was supposed to be my village, my native village, the same one I had once lived in as a boy and whose memory has never left me. Here I once knew every person, every house and stall, every reed, fence and barn. But why then did the road I was on seem completely alien?

During my wanderings had I lost the images of a distant reality, forgotten them and gradually replaced them with images of my own design? Or perhaps fantasies were appearing before me now, and my perception of reality did not correspond to this whimsical reality? After all, I was running a fever of at least thirty-nine degrees, and the surroundings could have been a figment of my feverish imagination.

I gathered a handful of snow, took off my shaggy hat, a present from some kind people, and pressed the snow against my forehead.

No, my feelings were quite normal. These strange houses and this deserted street really existed.

Then all my doubts were answered. A voice from the depths of my soul said:

'You really are in your native village, only the village is not the same as when you left it. The visions which brought you hundreds of kilometres to this, for you the dearest scrap of your fatherland, do not correspond to reality. That which you loved, that which you sought, no longer exists, or maybe if it does, then in a different form to that which was so incredibly near to you all these long years.'

Suddenly a new sharp, painful question arose: 'So why had I come?'

No one was expecting me in my native village, just as no one was expecting me in the countless other villages I had passed through. Even if anyone ever remembered me, it would be as one of the dead: everyone thought I was executed along with my father in 1930. The only people who knew that I was still alive were Petro Matviyovych and Hrytsko, who had sent me news of the death of my sisters and mother near Novosibirsk. But Hrytsko had died under the wheels of a train, and Petro Matviyovych no longer kept in touch with the village and, like me, was probably thought to be dead.

I had no family whatsoever left in the village. The boys with whom I had once teased dogs in the street probably wouldn't recognise me. Our property had probably fallen apart after twelve years and there was not a trace left of where to begin looking for it. The villagers I had known in my childhood had transformed into new beings, if you were to believe the newspapers, so the changes in people's souls must have been as drastic as the changes in the appearance of the village street.

I was seized with despair.

Why had I come then?

Maybe I would have to wander from house to house here too, until someone took me in for the night and fed me.

Just then I spied grandpa Maksym's old house. I recognised it at once. It had remained almost unchanged these past twelve years, having sunk only deeper into the ground and grown more moss on the roof. Suddenly I remembered. Hrytsko had told me of the fire which had destroyed the whole street, from grandpa Maksym's house to the fields.

So...

So, not everything was foreign and unknown to me. Something must have remained of my treasured past and it would link me to the present. Bridges still existed between the past and the present. The door I had entered many years ago was still there.

And so I proceeded to this door, as if approaching the past.

2

It was growing dark outside and a thick twilight filled the house. It was ineptly being fought off by the flickering light of a lamp. A dark woman was taking something out of the oven, while a grey-haired woman was sitting on a bench spinning, and a boy of seven or eight was napping at the table.

I knew none of them.

Again I felt uneasy, just as I had out in the fields, and again I felt that everything I saw was a dream, a hallucination, a figment of my imagination and sick mind.

"Good evening!" I said and grew frightened. I felt as if it wasn't me talking, as if someone else was sitting in my body, talking and moving on my behalf, and all I could do was hear his words and see his actions.

"Good evening!" replied three voices – two female and one a child's.

"Tell me, please," someone said with my lips, and I listened with interest to see what he would say, "tell me, please, did grandpa Maksym once live in this house."

"That he did."

"He's probably dead now, eh?"

"Yes, he passed away... Come in and sit down... Where do you know him from? You're not from the city, by any chance?"

"No, I've come a long way, from the front."

"From the front? Palazhka, ask him if he knows your Vasyl. Citizen, or should I say sir, have you ever met Vasyl Svyrydenko from Koshlayi?"

"What a question to ask," the younger woman mumbled unhappily. "It's not that small a world."

As she said this I noticed that I was still standing near the door (had I been invited to sit down or had I been dreaming?). I could feel the stuffiness, the extreme closeness in the room, and I felt delirious from my high temperature. I needed to put something cold to my forehead, a thought flashed through my mind and disappeared, burned by my flaming brain.

... How blinding and bright the lamp was. It made my eyes ache terribly... The young woman was saying something to me, but what?

I was now on the bench. The boy watched me from the table and his head became enormous and had split in half, so that I could see the white-washed walls in between the two halves. I heard distant voices – those of the occupants of the house and the person talking on my behalf, but they did not register in my mind.

Was I really in grandpa Maksym's house, or was I freezing somewhere out in the snow and merely hallucinating?

I could see the fields now. There was something black on the snow. It was me, my body, I recognised myself from far away and walked up – maybe I was still alive? I had to be lifted, to be carried into the village. I raised myself, lifted myself up, and collapsed with exhaustion. Snow had filtered under my collar and into my sleeves. I wanted to stand up and suddenly saw someone on the road. A pair of horses harnessed to a light sled, the left horse was spotted with some ridiculous colour. In the front of the sled was a boy on his knees lashing out with a whip, behind him the dark form of a woman wrapped in a large rug. They drew level with me and stopped the horses, the woman removed the rug from her head...

My mother's image appeared before me...

I had seen her last like this back in 1930. This was how I had imagined her while I was seeking her grave near Novosibirsk, this was how she appeared when I relived my childhood in reminiscences, this was how she appeared in my dreams.

Was I sleeping then?

If so, I had to wake up and find out where I was and what was wrong with me.

I made a terrible effort and something heavy seemed to fall from my head, my lungs could breathe more easily, and I could move, open my eyes. I looked up. My head cast a shadow on the table, the frightened boy stared at me, the women exchanged opinions as to what to do. The younger one said furiously:

"What a load of trouble! I'll have to fetch the village elder before he dies."

And the older one... I could swear I'd seen her somewhere before. I tried to remember when and where.

"He's deranged!" the younger one screamed. "Look how he stares!" And she raced outside, slamming the door.

The crash of the door brought on another wave of hot heavy turbidity, which inundated my consciousness.

3

In the morning when I woke up, or actually, as I was waking up, still half asleep, I heard a hushed conversation. I lay without moving and pretended to be asleep.

Soft and a trifle sad, the old woman's voice filled the room:

"Palazhka ran off for the village elder, meanwhile I lay him out on the bench, took his shoes off, put a pillow under his head and sat down thinking who it might be. A local or some traveller? Seems to be from far away, says he's from the front, but he speaks our tongue, though not quite the way we do in the country here. P'raps, I thought, he's a teacher or something? Someone's probably waiting for him at home, and he's lying ill here, unable to make it, and might even die.

"And where does he know old Maksym from? Maksym's been dead a long time now. Neither him nor any of his family left — some died in thirty-three, others made for the Donbas and around there. And no one knows who of Maksym's people have died and who is still roaming the country."

"It wasn't a time to count the deaths of others," another voice interrupted, unknown but with a pleasing ring to it.

"So I thought, maybe one of Maksym's people has returned home. Then I heard boots stamping in the entrance-hall. They came in. The village elder Karpo and Palazhka. Palazhka chirping like a bird around Karpo: 'Take him away, Mister Karpo, really, take him away!' I said to her: Palazhka, have you gone mad? And she replies: 'Aunt Mariana! Why did you put the cushion under his head?'"

132

"Nothing worse than living with strangers under the one roof," the resounding voice replied.

"Yeah, I said, I put it there, so what? And she turns to the village elder again: 'Search him, Uncle Karpo, maybe he's a Jew in hiding or a Soviet partisan. Maybe,' she says, 'he's got a pistol or a grenade?' Karpo thought and thought about it. Well, partisan or not, he should be frisked. 'Get up, lad,' he says. 'What the heck, Karpo,' I told him, 'come to your senses. The man's dying, and you're rousing him. No power on earth will be able to rouse him from his sleep soon, least of all a village elder.' Palazhka was fuming: 'Search his pockets, he'll have a gun for sure.' Karpo turned his pockets out: a pocket knife and ten Soviet roubles. He began looking for documents, but there wasn't even a sign of them. Palazhka was ecstatic: 'See, he's got no documents. I told you. Take him to the police, Uncle Karpo!' This time even he lost his patience. 'Don't prattle on, Palazhka,' he said. 'Those times have passed, when people ate people. Take him away... so that he'll die on the road...' And then I said to him: 'Here, I've found a book in his bag...'"

* * *

I was listening intently. Though I had never seen this Karpo before (was it really never?), I could vividly picture him taking the book, licking his finger, opening the book and slowly reading the letters of the title: 'The... Com... Complete... Works... of Fedor Sologub. See, Sologub. Shipovnik Publishers.' And then cruelly bending the sensitive pages and leaving finger marks on each one, he began to leaf through the book.

"They're poems of some sort," he said in surprise.

"Wait a minute, uncle, there's something written there," Palazhka interrupted his progress.

She took the book from the village elder's hands and, leafing back, found the words written in blue ink on page seventeen: '20.1.1942. From the library of Petro Matviyovych Oplenia,' she read out loud.

"What? Oplenia? Petro Matviyovych? Is that what it says?" the village elder asked with a start. "Here, give me the book! The damned light... It really looks like it's Petro Matviyovych's... Palazhka!" he ordered. "Run and fetch the doctor. This man's one of ours. If he's from Petro Matviyovych, then he's one of our people. He can't just be left to die!"

I made an uncertain movement and the story broke off, and with it the string of imaginary scenes I had conjured up and seen with my closed eyes. The women grew quiet.

They were looking at me, I assumed, though I couldn't feel their gazes on my face. Then, after a short pause, the older woman continued her story:

"I looked and looked at him, and said to Karpo: you know, Karpo, I said, he's a local. Perhaps even one of those for whom a funeral service has already been sung. Take, for example, Petro Matviyovych. Did anyone he was still alive? The man vanished like a stone plopping into water, and see, he's alive somewhere. You used to knock around with Serhiy, I said, the one nicknamed Remez[33], didn't you?

"'Yes,' he replied.

"And do you remember what he looked like in his youth?

"'Yes.'

"Look at the fellow, he remind you of anyone?

"He looked and let out a scream: "It's Serhiy, the spitting image of him!'"

... My heart beat madly, and my heart filled with a hitherto unknown joy. Meanwhile my muscles turned pleasantly powerless. A red and black ribbon with gold and green stars swam before my eyes. Someone had recognised me.

I knew then that all my nagging doubts of the previous day had been unfounded and that I really was in my native village. But what of it? What of it, if my whole being was filled only with weakness, when I didn't know whether my muscles would obey me, whether I could move, lift a hand, turn my head or open my eyes. Never have I felt such a sharp distinction between my consciousness and my foreign, superfluous body. It seemed as if my consciousness had condensed somewhere beyond the realms of space and time,

---

[33] In Ukrainian literally 'Titmouse'.

while the body lying on the bench was already not me, something belonging to me, but not me.

* * *

The woman continued talking, but I was unable to follow her. Then suddenly something seemed to hit me, uniting my detached body and consciousness, giving me control over my muscles. I had heard my mother's name mentioned:

"... And he said: we'll have to send someone to bring Kateryna from town tomorrow..."

Which Kateryna could they have been referring to? My mother? But she had died with my sisters somewhere near Novosibirsk. I had searched for their graves and was unable to find them!

"I advised him: 'Karpo, tell the driver not to tell her straight away, because she might die of joy...'"

I could hear someone sobbing, beginning to cry.

Yes, they were talking about my mother... Maybe she was already here in the house? Maybe it was her crying, as she heard the account of the older woman?

"Why are you crying, aunt Mariana? Come on, that's enough," said the one with a resounding voice, which was now muffled, constrained.

"Enough, you say, and you're crying yourself!" the older woman retorted through her tears.

I imagined her face, as she wiped away her tears and tried to smile.

"They said Kateryna perished in Siberia, but she returned. This one too, everyone knew, was executed with his father in 1930, but here he is – alive. And Oplenia's alive somewhere too. But none of mine are left, no one will ever return. They've all been murdered, tortured to death."

Her words gave way to sobbing.

"It's all right, Aunt Mariana, perhaps one of your relatives will come back."

I lay and listened, maintaining a calm carefree sleepy expression on my face. It's a difficult skill: to hide thoughts, to conceal sorrow

135

and joy. Hiding sorrow isn't too bad, we're used to it, but joy…
How hard it is to contain suppressed joy! With the feeling of joy
grew a fear that this was only a fleeting misunderstanding, that my
joy would end presently, that I would wake again and everything
would disintegrate and scatter. For those of us who are used only
to great suffering, are afraid to open ourselves to great joy; we
oppose it, hiding the depths of our souls from it, as we hide the
depths of our souls from everything which might befall us.

I turned over, opened my eyes, rose a little, and wanted to get
up, but felt I hadn't the strength.

"I'm sorry," I addressed the older woman, "for having come
uninvited and falling ill, causing you so much trouble."

"It's nothing, my dear son, it's nothing," the older woman said
affectionately.

I tried to get up again.

"Stay in bed," the younger woman ran up to me: not the one
who'd been here yesterday, but another one – beautiful, friendly,
intelligent, the owner of the resounding voice.

I noticed smeared traces of tears on her face and thought not
without satisfaction that these tears were provoked by her feelings
for me.

"Lie down, you mustn't get up."

I protested vehemently:

"Sorry, but I feel quite well…"

"It's good that you're better. But if only you knew the
temperature you had yesterday evening. And your pulse, God, what
a pulse. So uneven, intermittent. It's amazing that your heart
survived!"

I realised that she was the doctor.

4

That same day, after I had regained a little of my strength and
had some lunch, I recognised in Mariana a distant relative of ours.
I also learned that my mother had returned from Siberia in 1935
and now lived in a town several kilometres away, where she
worked as a cleaner in a hospital. After this I was forced to reply to
Aunt Mariana's questions, and, like it or not, told her that I had

evaded execution more than once. At that moment a boy, Palazhka's Kolia, raced into the house.

"She's coming!" he yelled happily.

"Who?"

"His mother."

Taking advantage of the absence of the doctor, who had gone home to eat, I threw something over my shoulders and with Aunt Mariana's help went out onto the porch. What I saw will forever remain impressed in my mind, and forever reinforce my belief in the extraordinary and miraculous: a sled came flying down the wide snow-covered street. It was pulled by two horses. The left one was mottled, funny, small; a boy was kneeling in the front of the sled and cracking his whip; behind him sat a woman wrapped in a large rug.

This was the enactment of my hallucination or dream of the day before.

The dream had become reality.

But I wasn't lying in the fields, I was standing on the porch beside Mariana. Only my mother, when she rose in the sled, was small, with grey hair which showed from under the rug, with wrinkles around her eyes, her face yellow and eyes faded like an autumn sky, eyes filled with tears and a helpless happiness. Only my mother looked so different to the one I had dreamed of and imagined...

But this was my mother...

Perhaps great joy is so intense only because it bears a trace of sadness.

THE HOUSE ON THE CLIFF

*Excerpt of sequel to
'Because Deserters Are Immortal'*

MY NAME

1

Never in my life, not before nor after, had I been held in such high esteem as in the spring and summer of 1942. And never had my individuality meant so little.

Whether it was on the cement floor of a prison cell or at a desk in the institute auditorium – I always occupied a place I had chosen for myself.

In the examination room, or in the dock, or in a street fight at night – no matter what unpleasant, tragic or tragicomical circumstances I found myself in – the matter was always decided by my knowledge, my conduct, my manner of reacting. Often it was only a single calculated gesture, an expressive look, an apt word.

And if it wasn't this, but the intervention of a friend which saved the day, then hadn't the ability to find loyal, devoted friends been a good quality of mine?

For twelve years I had lived under constant strain and continual restriction of freedom. The whole time I always had to fight someone, to run away from somewhere, and to change everything – from my hairstyle to my name, and mostly I had to keep quiet, so that no one would guess that I had a past.

Now all this had changed. It was a time of relaxation. All the dangers which had surrounded me these past years were absent.

The Soviet activists left behind to carry out underground work sat quietly, not daring to even let drop a word about the happy times of their collective paradise.

The network of agents, provocateurs and informers destroyed by the passing front had yet to be re-established.

2

Two Soviet paratroopers who had wandered into the village Velyki Khashchi had been stabbed to death with pitchforks by the villagers.

141

The Germans were still a long way away. The small neighbouring village of Koshlayi, located far from the highway and the railway line, and hidden behind a marshy wood, had not been visited by them at all, so that the old women there, who usually never ventured beyond their own fields, except for visiting our village or Vokhre once or twice a year for parish fairs, these old women still had no idea what a German looked like.

Armies crossed our region without clashing: one lot retreated, each soldier looking out for himself, hungry, unshaven, covered in dirt and lice. A new lot arrived – well-fed, clothes ironed, clean-shaven and faultlessly proper.

When I told the villagers of the looting and violence I had witnessed, no one believed me.

True, it was a reminder that the world was not just our village, we had a *Stuetzpunktleiter* – a 'saintly commandant' who neither smoke nor drank, nor fought nor swore, and didn't even have an interpreter by his side. He reacted to everything with the same words: '*Gut, gut!*' ate potatoes splashed with oil, and when I brought him a freshly-caught two kilogram pike once, he grew embarrassed and refused to take it.

Instead of dilapidated state flats, with dark smelly hallways, we were surrounded by village houses which were clean and bright.

Instead of the motley mixture of crims and militiamen, workers and public servants, revamped 'has-beens' and Party members, pupils and students, there were staid villagers here, all uniform, resembling one another, or so it seemed to me, in their lifestyles and interests.

In place of friends, instead of books – there was no one and nothing. There was only serenity.

Just as a peasant, on arriving in a large city, stood lost, forgetting where he had to go and what matters he had to attend to, so too I had become lost upon finding myself amid this great serenity.

In my years of wandering, I often recalled our house on the bend of the river, on a cliff overlooking a stretch of water where I had once paddled about in the weeds, our village street in early spring, when water dripped from the straw thatch of the roofs. But never – for so I had been taught – never had I uttered, neither aloud nor in whispers, either the name of my village or my own real name.

True, twice I had come across compatriots, who had known me...

And also once I had uttered my real name to a friend. But this had been later, under German occupation.

And now I was living in my native village and being called by my own name. It was my name, which was in fact the prime reason for the ingratiating respect I received, and which I abhorred.

The whole secret was that I was my grandfather's grandson, and my father's son. And that I was now the owner of the best farmstead for miles around, which nestled atop a cliff. The property had once belonged to a landlord. My grandfather had bought it for a song from some impoverished landowners. People said the house had once been set in a park with alleys, arbours and grottos. When I had been small, I had once found a piece of a plaster cupid buried in the riverbank.

Grandfather had chopped down the park, pulled out the stumps and made a giant vegetable garden. But at the base of the cliff and on the cliffs which surrounded the house in a semi-circle, everywhere where it was impossible to plough, the trees had remained. And something else remained too, something unfathomable, which reminded one of Gogol's quaint landowners or Turgenev's nests of gentlefolk.

Therefore the land was severed from the collective farm and the house was turned into a sanatorium. And at the start of summer each year, when the duck season began, Soviet aristocrats from Chernihiv and even Kyiv congregated here with their rifles, chauffeurs, dogs and mistresses.

And now all this – I don't mean the dogs and mistresses of the Party member hunters, of course – all this was now mine.

In the several months since I had arrived here I had not had the chance nor the need to reveal myself in any way. No one knew whether I was smart or stupid, whether I was kind or nasty, whether I had talent or not. Though no one was particularly interested.

All they knew was that while still a boy I had been sentenced to be shot together with my father and had somehow managed to escape this fate. That my mother had been deported to Siberia and had also returned.

But above all was the fact that I was the son of Serhiy Remez.

143

And then several dozen mothers – it was an epidemic – thought of marrying their daughters off to me. I might even have married one of them, but the girl I liked most left voluntarily to work in Germany. As for the others, well... their mothers were far too importunate.

The formerly dispossessed peasants saw in me a representative of their class and felt a certain affinity toward me. The Soviet activists weren't far behind in displaying their goodwill, for the possibility of becoming related to me would have returned them to the ranks of the village aristocracy. And they wanted so much to be able to issue orders again!

The worst thing was that because of the rivalry, each discredited their real and imagined rivals, so that even if only half of what they told me was true, I was scared stiff of going near the girls.

There are no secrets in a village.

I found it hard to differentiate between the girls: there were seven Marusias, five Halias, three Paraskas, two Katerynas, and the rest all began with 'o' – Odarka, Oryshka, Olena, Oksenia, Onyska and Olha. Anyhow, after a while I knew all there was to know about each one of them.

For example, Olena wore a long skirt because her legs were covered with incurable scabs, and one of the Marusias always wore a kerchief, because she was 'covered in scabs, like a necklace', to use the words of the writer Kotliarevsky.

One day I met a nice girl named Halia (not from our village, but from Koshlayi) on the bridge and had chatted with her for fifteen minutes. That evening Aunt Uliana, our neighbour, dropped by to see us, as if by chance, and told us that Stepan Stepanovych, Halia's father, wasn't really her father at all. There followed a story worthy of Maupassant, which I will perhaps try to recreate one day. Vasyl Dumka, an old bachelor friend of mine, advised me to go for his sister, Oryshka. But in Oryshka's own words, she had 'passed through two classes and a third corridor', and everything she had learnt had been forgotten after working at the collective farm. What could I ever find in common with such a girl, what could we ever talk about?

Karpo, the village elder, tried to convince me that the best girl around was his niece, Kateryna. True, she was an intelligent,

144

beautiful and friendly girl. The only thing was that after the family had been dispossessed she had lived for two or three years in a children's home in Chernihiv, and there the boys had done with her as they pleased. I did not see this as any fault of hers, for what could she have known then, being only ten, but people said she still continued to act in the same way when the Red Army had been stationed in the village. One did not want to believe this, but there were no secrets in a village, so it had to be true. 'Damaged goods' Aunt Uliana called her.

She had two daughters of her own: Marusia, the older one, was not so beautiful, but she was cheerful, lively and nice, while the younger one, Paraska, had severe classical features, but was devoid of any expression. Uliana often helped my mother around the house or sent her younger daughter to help. When I asked Vasyl Dumka why she wasn't trying to tempt me with the older daughter first, Vasyl replied that the older daughter had worked a season in Kyiv and had not returned intact.

Kindrat, the settled Gypsy from Koshlayi, did not have the courage to offer me his daughter's hand in marriage, and came to see mother on several occasions to convince her that I would never be able to marry in the village because there wasn't anyone equal to me here, so perhaps I could take in his Nastia to work as a maid. Someone might snitch on him to the Germans, at least then his daughter would be saved.

The school principal, Chuyko (now he had become the co-operative manager), who had neither a daughter, nor a niece, suggested I marry his star pupil. Plain, freckle-faced, she wasn't the type boys looked at twice. But after she and I had exchanged several sentences, I found out how well-read, witty and faultlessly intelligent she was. Only once again she could not become my wife: her father and uncles belonged to those who had dispossessed us.

I don't believe, can't and won't believe, that parents' sins and crimes are passed on to their children and grandchildren; for me a person is a closed, finished, individual entity, with whom everything begins and ends (the fact that voluntary and forced actions of people serve as accelerators or brakes in the eternal chain of motives has nothing to do with taking responsibility for the sins

145

of one's forebears); but if only I had met this girl somewhere under different circumstances, in a different milieu. As it was, she lived in a family belonging to the circle which I detested.

I asked Vasyl whether there were any other sharp girls in the village, perhaps engineers, students or actresses. He said there was one he knew of and the following Sunday introduced me to black-haired Olia. She guffawed louder than need be and really looked more like a worker from a confectionary factory than a recent literature graduate.

Because I had been living outside Ukraine since I was thirteen, I was most curious to learn what was being taught then in Ukrainian tertiary institutions. And I asked her:

"What did you study in Ancient Ukrainian literature?"

She thought a while and replied: "'The Lay of Igor's Campaign'."

"What else?"

"'The Song of the Nibelungs'."

"That isn't Ukrainian literature, is it?"

"Who cares..."

Obviously she belonged to the same group as the girl in our class who, when asked what 'monogamy' was, replied: '*Mnogodamy*[34] is when one man has several women.' This didn't suit me either.

So I went about alone, as if in agreement with the wife of the collective-farm accountant, Maryna Pavlivna, who tried to convince me that I was still young, only twenty-five, and that there was nowhere to hurry; only village youths once married at eighteen, while I could wait another two years or so. Besides, these were uncertain times. This advice was based on Maryna Pavlivna's simple arithmetic, which had nothing to do with accounting: her fourteen-year-old blue-eyed Zinochka would reach the age of consent in two years.

By the middle of summer I had become accepted in the village and felt at home in the company of the village youths. Apart from the immutable Vasyl Dumka, I also made friends with the giant Dmytro, the village elder's nephew, and rekindled my old friendship from school days with Korniy Bovdur and Kyrylo

---

[34] Russian, literally 'many ladies'.

Oplenia, a relative of the Petro Oplenia who had once taken me in.

Korniy, Kyrylo, myself and another coeval of ours who was married – this was all that now remained of our group (classes were called groups then) of twenty-seven or twenty-eight boys with whom I had attended school from group one to group six. Several had been deported with their parents to the polar wastes after the dispossession of the peasants, others had died of hunger or joined the ranks of the *shpana* and died somewhere. Two had been executed in 1937, one was doing ten years in a concentration camp in Pechora Region and the rest were in the Soviet Army – if one assumed they had not fallen in battle or perished in concentration camps.

Those of us who were alive didn't even mention them. And whereas before my connections with the criminal underworld and hooligans had weakened and ties had been broken because of studies at the institute, so now too the black earth surrounding me seemed to change my being: I simply couldn't become absorbed in the books from the school library which I tried to read, and even Sologub's book, which I had brought with me, was no longer opened. The poems which I tried to recite to myself sounded distant and failed to move my soul. They seemed obliterated from overuse and there was nowhere to get new ones from.

When at the end of summer the young Doctor Les, also one of the dispossessed, returned to the village – he fancied telling jokes, and loved women and drink – I finally stopped feeling an alienation to the village way of life.

And yet I still lacked something. Our country must be the only one in the world where mateship still exists, where one can find true mateship between a boy and a girl.

I found a substitute in the form of companionship with people who were different in spirit and on a different cultural level.

But I needed to find a substitute, at least a substitute, for the second type of relationship too.

3

One Sunday I noticed an unfamiliar girl in the colourful crowd of young people.

Grey-eyed, with slim, maybe even too fine features, she had ashen hair. She was dressed in a grey 'city' dress, which strangely suited the colour of her eyes and hair. She had an air of refined elegance, which I had not seen for a long time.

The girl walking by her side, plump Odarka, was obviously a friend.

Neither Vasyl nor Korniy were nearby, and only Dmytro was standing next to me – he was far too young to know who this girl was and where she was from. All the same I asked him:

"Dmytro, who's that?"

"Vasyl Riabchyn's Odarka."

"No, the one with her."

"Some girl from Koshlayi or maybe Vokhre."

It was obvious that this grey-eyed girl with the slender waist and artistic fingers did not match Dmytro's idea of beauty.

Village girls and boys know each other from childhood and, therefore, with the appearance of a stranger known to only a few of them, it occurred to no one to introduce the new person. But this grey-eyed girl was from the city (it was hard to imagine her being from Koshlayi or Vokhre), and in order to make her acquaintance, I needed an intermediary. I was about to turn to Odarka for help when Les slapped me on the shoulder and uttered some witty obscenity. I immediately tried to alter my intentions and attempted to take him aside, so that he wouldn't see her.

Then someone brought out a bottle of home-made vodka and we all piled into someone's house where snacks were laid out for us.

Later it grew dark and I tried in vain to spot the grey dress in the grey twilight.

During the following week I didn't think about her at all, but on Saturday night I dreamed that she was a porcelain 'Lancere' statuette which I was holding in the palm of my hand.

Of all the candidates I had been advised to woo so far, I had dreamt of none. Not even the doctor who had gone off to Germany.

The next Sunday I recognised her from afar, though she wasn't wearing her ashen dress, and instead had a corset with 'whisker' – she seemed even more beautiful. I walked up to her and without any introduction, said: "I knew you'd be coming today."

"How?"

148

"Because I dreamt of you."

She laughed. Odarka swung around and disappeared.

A lively conversation ensued about everything and nothing. Vasyl Dumka was not around. Korniy Bovdur kept a close watch on us from a distance. I called out to him, but he did not join us: either he hadn't heard me or didn't dare.

We left the group and wandered along a path close to the river: from the small bridge, where an accordion was playing, all the way to the old barn. And then to the bridge and back to the barn again. I learnt that she was from Vokhre, had finished ten grades, but hadn't gone anywhere because of the war – and just as well. Her father was a railways official. She was friends with Odarka from school – Odarka had gone to school in Vokhre, because our local school only had nine grades.

"And you?"

"I'm one of those who has returned to his native thatch."

She didn't understand what I meant and began to explain that their roof was covered in iron, not straw thatch.

Our house, which had six rooms, was roofed with iron too, but I didn't tell her that: it was obvious that the girl didn't know who I was. And it was better to keep it like that. It was exactly what I needed.

Let her judge me, let her treat me as I myself deserved to be treated, and not because of my name or the shadow of my father and his house on the cliff. And I said to her:

"There is more poetry in a straw thatch roof. I once read somewhere that American millionaires built arbours under straw."

Then we talked about millionaires, arbours and poetry.

She knew the names of a dozen or so Soviet poets: Bezymensky, Svetlov, Edouard Bagritsky, Semion Kirsanov, Mikhail Golodny, Ilya Selvinsky, Iosif Utkin... She was especially fond of Bezymensky.

And she read me an excerpt from 'Tragic Night':

A serene Ukrainian night.
Clear skies. Stars shining.
The still air has no desire
To awaken. The silvery leaves
Of poplars glimmer in the dark...

The rest was somewhat different, but still nice:

> *Laugh, oh moon, don't taunt me,*
> *From your heavenly well so deep...*

I told her that the beginning was really nice, only it wasn't Bezymensky, but Alexander Pushkin.

"No way, it's definitely Bezymensky!" she insisted.

"Believe me, it's Pushkin. Do you want to make a bet?"

"All right. I'll show you my Bezymensky. Come to my place."

"Sure, and I'll bring my Pushkin."

The invitation to visit her was a real triumph for me. Or perhaps she really knew who I was?

Until now I had talked to her without mentioning my name and never asking hers. This in no way hindered our conversation: if need be I can talk with a person without calling them by their name or even without using the polite or familiar form of address. But now I needed to know whom I would be visiting. I asked her indirectly:

"Who shall I look out for?"

She didn't understand.

"Well, whom shall I ask in Vokhre?"

"Ask whoever you like. Everyone there knows Svitlana Volkonska. And who shall I be expecting?"

"Me."

"So who shall I tell mother is coming?"

"Me!"

I turned it all into a joke, but she became visibly displeased and began to say goodbye, saying she still had to visit Odarka to return the clothes she had borrowed and put her dress back on.

"I met Svitlana Volkonska," I reported to Vasyl Dumka. "What a beautiful girl! A real princess... And her surname..."

"Not bad, she's a pretty piece."

"I'm off to visit her tomorrow."

Vasyl looked at me with the same expression on his face, as Korniy Bovdur had had an hour earlier, and said sorrowfully:

"You're not acting like a true friend. She's Korniy's girl. She's been coming here because of him. I hope you're not like Les, to win girls from your own friends."

150

"If that's the case, I can remain at home."

I remembered how our school friendship with Korniy had finished after Hrytsko Smovzyk and I had attacked him from behind and beaten him up for something – I can't remember what for now.

Success in life did not come easily to Korniy. He was an average student. A furious step-mother tried to finish him off at home. While several of our coevals had finished tertiary institutes and technical colleges, he hadn't gone further than a factory apprenticeship and worked as a fitter. Their house was burnt down in the great fire which destroyed our whole street. His family had all died except for his married older step-sister, with whom he now lived, sharing the house with her numerous children.

All he had was his slender waist and dark-brown hair, and his matte, beautifully sculpted face.

It wasn't so easy for him to marry someone. Unless he went to live de facto with some Russian woman. And so I repeated my peremptory decision once more:

"If that's the case, I can stay put at home."

4

Two, perhaps three weeks went by.

The mornings became fresh and serenely sorrowful – the evenings were clear.

But during the day the sun still burned with its summer strength.

Our close friend, Halyna Petrovna from Vokhre, raced into our house one day without a word of greeting and blurted out:

"Don't let him marry her!" And she collapsed into a chair.

"Who?" mother asked, handing her some water.

The woman gestured in my direction and brought the glass to her mouth.

"With whom?" mother asked.

"With Svetka – ooh, I ran so fast, let me finish drinking... With Yashka Volkonsky's Svetka."

I was flabbergasted.

You couldn't keep anything secret in a village, it was as bad as the NKVD: one's actions became common knowledge before they had even been performed.

This was probably the reason why there were no big crimes in villages: in the five or six surrounding villages, perhaps even twice that number, no one could remember a single murder from way back – if one didn't count village kangaroo courts over horse-thieving, the first communards and the present paratroopers.

Of course people stole. And each theft was remembered for decades by the people:

"Your father stole my grandfather's axe."

"And your mother pilfered potatoes from our garden."

I stood there speechless, not knowing what to say.

Meanwhile Halyna Petrovna had caught her breath, smoothed her hair in place, wiped the sweat from her face and began a prosecutor's tirade:

"Why didn't any of you at least ask me what that Svetka was all about?"

She hurled staccato sentences at us, and each was like a verdict:

"She smokes.

"And drinks.

"She gulps down methylated spirits.

"She swears at her own mother.

"When she goes off to town she not only paints her lips, but also does her toenails.

"She's educated, intelligent, reads books, knows German – but just you ask her if she's ever washed the floor or cooked a decent meal. There's no one worse than that Svetka in the whole of Vokhre!

"You could at least have asked me, before sending matchmakers."

"What matchmakers are you talking about?" my mother was perplexed.

"Oh, so he decided off his own bat, without even asking his mother, eh?"

"No one's been sending matchmakers anywhere," I said, although it sounded rather unconvincing.

"What do you mean? That old witch Volkonska has been

bragging to all and sundry that Serhiy Remez's son has been round to their place to ask for her daughter's hand in marriage."

"When did he come?" I asked in disbelief.

"Yesterday evening."

"But I haven't been in Vokhre for over a month now!"

"People say they saw you."

Something strange was happening here which I was unable to fathom.

I can't remember how I justified myself back then, but from that day on I decided to move to the city: there one didn't have to be so careful about what one said and did, and there no one would remember an unguarded remark uttered ten years previously or censure one for talking half an hour or so to a girl who accidentally happened to have loose morals. In the city one didn't have to worry about 'tainting' grandfather's good name. My name would mean nothing there, and I would be judged on my own merits.

Almost a year later, when I was working in the editorial office of a non-existent newspaper (only two issues had ever been published and a third was being typeset), I dropped by the village one Sunday to visit my mother.

Young people were milling around the church with no cupola.

From the festive mood of the crowd I guessed it was a wedding.

I jumped down off the cart and walked up to the church, rapturously greeted by Vasyl Dumka and Korniy Bovdur.

Few people married in the village after Easter: usually the ceremony took place in autumn or outside of Lent.

Must be someone from the station in Vokhre, I thought...

"We're waiting for the bride," said Vasyl Dumka. "She's marrying the policeman from Koshlayi. You see, the village elder wanted to send her off to Germany, so this is how she is saving herself. She was a neat little girl, Yakiv Volkonsky's Svitlana was. You wanted to visit her one time."

"Well I went and saw her," Korniy added. "And several times at that. And you know," he turned to me, "I thought, what should I tell her? After all, who was I? I had no kith or kin. Plain old Korniy Bovdur – no one's ever heard of him. No house, no nothing. I live

153

with my sister, and even she isn't related by blood.

"But you have a house with a tin roof, and enough trees on your land to build a fine house, and even more than one. And you had a mother. And a sow, and a cow. You were drinking buddies with the regional chief and were on first name terms with all the interpreters. And you had an education. And a name known throughout the whole district.

"So I told her that I was you..."

EMPRESSES

1

It is hard to tell what it was really like in the Neolithic Age during the Trypillia period in Ukraine. Perhaps a matriarchal society really did exist back then, or perhaps it was merely the fantasy of some archaeologist.

In historical times Ukraine had been ruled by women twice. The first time was during the Russian Empire, when two Catherines reigned, two Annas and a merry Elizabeth, and the second time was within our memory, twenty years ago.

But the second period differed somewhat from the first: the empresses did not rule one after the other, but all at once. There were at the very least several thousand of them, and the reign of each lasted a mere two years and was confined to a certain district or town. None of them had as many dresses as Elizabeth, or as many lovers as Catherine.

But the essence of the matter was the same: vodka, soldiers, free love...

And I was the only courtier.

And here is how it happened.

* * *

Had I told this story a hundred years ago I would have had to write how the driver Stepan had come for me at dawn, how the forest hay smelt under the sacking, how the low morning sun blinded us, and how mother tried to dissuade me from the journey at the last moment – as if I was going forever and not just for one day, and not just to a town fifteen kilometres away, but somewhere beyond the bounds of this world.

All this would have occupied no less than ten pages. Then, for another twenty pages I would have written an account of the journey, during which nothing at all happened. Village elder Karpo steered the horses while the driver dozed idly, and I lay back and tried to pretend that I was six years old and travelling to town with my grandfather for the first time in my life. Grandfather had considered it his duty to take gifts each year in the form of vegetables and fruit to the old lady from whom he had bought his farmstead for a quarter of its price. The old woman had a daughter and a grand-daughter – perhaps there had been other members of the family, but I never noticed them. The grand-daughter was a year or two older than me, and I quite vividly pictured her long, thin, untanned legs, her skirt which reached way above her knees and the white underpants which took every opportunity to peer out from under that skirt. I didn't seem to remember any other details.

Anyhow, I didn't exert myself too much to remember much more. Oblomov had laid in bed thinking, but during my stay in the village I had become so lazy, that I could no longer think.

The district council office was located in an indistinct building in a side street, and met us more than ungraciously. On the fence near the door we saw a half-metre high printed declaration with the innocent headline:

'Attention! Attention!'

We were then informed that on the morning of this day a hundred men had been executed on the outskirts of town. This was in retaliation for the death of a German soldier murdered by unknown criminals near the town. At the end there was a promise to execute a hundred more of the local civilian population for every German that was killed. Nothing was said about the fact that killings of this kind were the result of the activities of local Chekists, left behind for this very purpose, or the work of Soviet paratroopers.

First of all, I envied the population of N. of whom only ten were being executed for each German killed. I wondered whether these numbers were decided by the local command, or whether they came from Berlin itself, from the Fuhrer?

A hundred in Ukraine, but only ten in Russia. Or perhaps it was ten last year, and a hundred today? Or perhaps everything depended on the whim of the district commander?

I remembered the joke of the merry SS officers who had once led us out to be executed, without even asking us our names.

And the Russian village where it was rumoured that a hundred muzhiks had been executed after Red Senka had stripped the skin from the back and stomach of a live German...

156

...Perhaps it was best to remain in the village and not to travel anywhere...?

Until now I had not thought about the reason for our journey. Uncle Karpo had said to me: 'We're going to town tomorrow.' Well, and here we were.

I went along for a change of scenery and to stretch my legs, for when a person remains for too long in the same place, they become like a willow stake driven into damp ground – it sends out roots and becomes immovable. I was also attracted by the possibility of making new friends and to meet people with whom I could discuss things besides rods and pegs, for example about Maupassant and Schopenhauer. There was also the possibility of meeting old friends. I only had one friend with a capital 'F'. There were about ten loyal and sincere friends, counting the girls I knew, and there would have been close to fifty good acquaintances. And since most of them differed little in age, temperament and social standing to me, there was always the possibility of unexpected encounters.

"This is the man I told you about," the village elder introduced me to one of the district council officials.

Only now did I learn the reason he had brought me to town. He had thought, you see, that the village had to have its own man in the district council, and I, it seemed to him, was the best candidate for such a position. He had mentioned me to the district chief earlier, when the man had visited our village.

The fellow who was meant to be my patron (and who, I later learned, was a very minor figure in the new hierarchy), announced that the district chief would be in his office only after lunch, and that meanwhile he would give me a small examination.

The examination went something like this:

"Do you have a diploma?"

"No, I haven't."

"What about a higher education?"

"No. I'm a correspondence student."

"How are you at book-keeping?"

"Not too bad."

"How is your German?"

"Poor."

"Hm... Without a knowledge of the German language, without

157

a higher education, you won't have much luck – even the courier here has a higher education. You can offer your services to the town's police. They take any riff-raff they can get."

I knew neither who the fellow was, nor what position he held, but if it wasn't for Uncle Karpo, whom I didn't want to suffer any unpleasantness, I would have smashed his face in. Or perhaps it was the Ukrainian national trait coming out in me under the influence of my environment: to accumulate insults inside of me instead of reacting to them.

I merely asked him as politely as I could:

"So why aren't you in the police force yet?"

Hour dragged on after hour in fruitless waiting. Only at the end of the working day were we able to talk with another character, who said that the district chief would not be coming in that day: his mother-in-law had died and he was carousing at the wake. But as an aside, he added that neither the district chief, nor the district council, nor the police had any clout: all authority was in the hands of the Germans. And the Germans were manipulated by the four female interpreters: Sonia, Bronia, Veronika and Leonida Leonivna.

The oldest among them, Leonida Leonivna, exercised the greatest power, for she knew all the European languages and lived with a German named Herr Oberst Baron von Trippenbach.

But the others could also do whatever they liked.

As an example, one of the female teachers wanted to go to N.

"To N. ...?" I asked.

"Yes, to N. She has a son there in a prisoner-of-war camp. No matter how much she pleaded through the district council, nothing came of it. Then she turned to Veronika, gave her a chicken – and she had her pass almost immediately. She's off tomorrow."

He knew neither the name nor the address of the teacher. Some teacher from some village. On the other hand he knew the interpreter's address very well.

Leaving the driver with the horses in the district council yard, we set off: I to seek out Veronika, the village elder to the wake of the chief's mother-in-law.

Each street in the town had three names: our Ukrainian one, the Soviet name and the German one. I could find my way around at least thirty cities in the Soviet Union without any trouble, only my native Chernihiv Region remained a blind spot to me: I had avoided it for ten years so as not to encounter people who might know me and recognise me.

However, I reached Veronika's place without too much trouble: grandfather and I had once travelled along this very street. And the closer I came to her house, the more vivid my childhood memories became. Here was the same building, with columns entwined with wild grape, and on the left, behind the mulberries, stood the sunken old shed into which they had once been forced to move. The high fence of cast-iron bars, interwoven with the figures of wolfhounds and riders (probably a masterpiece of the old casting industry) was no more: obviously it had been salvaged for use as scrap iron. In its place stood a low lattice fence, clearly recently constructed, and from behind which, in place of flower beds, grew green knot-grass and geraniums.

I entered the yard like an old friend. Where were they: in the shed or the house proper?

The shed stood with no glass in the windows and the door was nailed over with boards. So, they were in the house.

I ascended the high porch, passed between the tatty columns, and knocked on the glass door. Once, twice... The third time I caught sight of a female form in the depths of the house which spied me in the doorway and called out in Russian:

"Veronika, it's for you!" And disappeared.

Soon Veronika appeared too. She was wearing a small robe under which I could imagine her long straight legs and completely flat chest. Her face was washed-out, wilted – could she really have been only twenty-seven?

Wordlessly I bowed with a smile-like grimace.

She replied dryly in Russian:

"What do you want?"

"Here's what I want: a teacher from here is going off to N. I have two close friends in N. and I wanted to give each of them a small message. This would be very advantageous for both me and the teacher: she would have somewhere to stay, and people to show her everything and tell her everything. And I would get news from my friends."

"So what's the problem?"

"I wanted to know where I could find this teacher, or at least what her name is... I was told the interpreter Veronika had gotten a pass for her."

"Your source of information isn't accurate: interpreter Bronia got this woman a pass, not me."

She neither asked me inside, nor asked me to sit down on the stone benches on the porch, showing no interest at all in me.

And so I asked:

"Listen, Veronika, do you really not recognize me, or are you just playing dumb?"

"Why shouldn't I recognize you? I heard that you had returned. But I see no reason to talk with you on familiar terms."

2

I never abandon my intentions at the first failure. For that to happen I have to go through two or three failures.

And so I went off to see interpreter Bronia.

Bronia lived at the opposite end of town, across the river. What had made her live so far away!

Giving me her workmate's address, Veronika's voice was openly disdainful. But I don't think there was a thing in the world toward which Veronika would not have acted disdainfully.

She had been the same back then when she had worn her lily-white underpants and had tried to convince me that I was a muzhik, and that she was a young lady. (And I had replied to her that I was no muzhik, but in fact a Cossack, and she couldn't be aristocracy, for they were all at the bottom of the Black Sea.)

'It must be somewhere here,' I thought, when I reached a large half-destroyed orchard from which emanated the astringent fragrance of fresh false acacia leaves. Perhaps Veronika had said something to me about this orchard and I had forgotten her words, only vestiges remained in my subconsciousness.

There was an empty woodshed and a chicken coop, a small city house in the middle of the yard...

I was certain I would be received differently here. I slapped the gate latch several times – nothing. I ascended the porch and knocked on the door. Something seemed to answer from inside, and taking this sound for an invitation to enter, I stepped inside.

The door from the entrance hall to a room in the house was open. In the middle of the room there was a large table laid. Upon it stood a samovar, large jugs, two bowls – one with pickled tomatoes, the other with some sort of leftovers, three bottles of drink, and then more skillets, plates, glasses, knives and forks – dirty and clean, empty and full – everything was in a jumble. A pillow lay under the table, and at the table, facing me, sat an olive-skinned, drunk, hook-nosed girl.

Neither I, nor any of my friends, not even Pashka Orlan, had ever drunk on our own. Only once had I seen a man drinking alone, and that was in Moscow when Isaac Finkelstein introduced me to some Russian literary figure, and I, having arranged a meeting over the phone, turned up at the literateur's home.

Wearing a Russian fur cap with ear flaps, the literateur was hunched over a bucket, vomiting. The room smelt of spirits and vomit. Kitchen spirit-lamps lay strewn about the floor.

"Ah, it's you," the literateur raised his head and recognized me. "Well, start reading." We had agreed that I would read him some of my poetical attempts.

"Well, I... perhaps another time..."

"Read, I said...!"

And I had to read. I thought it sacrilege to share my cherished thoughts and imagery with this animal.

I was saved by his neighbour, who burst in screaming:

"On the spirits again! At least you might try to put some sense in his head, young man. Ooh, the layabout, the medal-beggar!"

And while she retrieved her empty spirit-lamp, cursing the whole time, I had made a quick exit into the passage.

But here before me was a young girl, and not some famous literary figure.

"Good health to you!" I said for want of something to say.

The girl – she was very thin, delicate in appearance and, despite her cloudy eyes, still quite beautiful – looked at me and said decisively:

"I know why you're here."

"Why?"

"You've come to..." she stammered, quickly poured herself a glass, emptied it, and only then finished: "You've come for... the same reason you all come here."

The thought flashed through my mind that instead of interpreter Bronia, I had come upon a refuge of ill repute – one of probably countless such places now dotting the cities of Ukraine.

"But... I was looking for interpreter Bronia... in regards to a personal matter," I wanted to excuse myself, but this was not the place for excuses.

"You all come looking for interpreter Bronia," the girl said fiercely and stretched her hand out for the bottle again. "I know you all, what you start with, and what it all leads to. You all knew my parents, and are eager to help, and feel sorry for me, and won't go to the Gestapo with a denunciation. But I need to pay for your silence... If it had been the Germans, I'd understand, but you are all ours, our people...!"

She broke down sobbing.

Then she wiped away her tears, filled her glass again, checked to see how much was left in the bottle, and poured me a drink.

"Scoff it down! And go on your way. Come around some other time."

I downed the drink and almost had a fit of coughing: it was distilled millet alcohol, at least eighty proof.

"He'll be here soon..." she again shook with sobs. "If only you knew how ugly... how ugly his body is...!"

The glass rattled against her teeth and the strong liquid dribbled down her chin and onto the table.

The black hair, the aquiline nose, this solitary residence where there was no family – everything was clear as day. The only thing I didn't know was whom she was expecting.

Also I wasn't sure how much she'd had to drink. She had downed two glasses in my presence, but she had been quite drunk on my arrival. I moved the unfinished bottle away.

"Give it here!" she commanded, stretching out her hand.

"That's enough," I said curtly, grabbing her hand. And then I bent over toward her: "What's the matter, do you want to burn up completely?"

"So what if I do! What's... it... to... you..."

162

The last glass had made her completely drunk and her tongue found it difficult to get around the words.

But she had already forgotten about the bottle and hugging me in a fit of drunken empathy, began to mumble something indistinct which sounded like Yiddish. Suddenly she stopped in mid sentence, her face became white as chalk, her eyes rolled up into her sockets, her body slipped down onto the chair and would have fallen to the ground had I not caught her.

I never imagined that such a small body could be so heavy. Or perhaps it was just that my muscles were flabby after several long months of idleness, during which I had fought no one, chased no one, and had run away from no one.

Struggling, I dragged her outside. She seemed to come to, but couldn't stand on her feet. I removed my jacket, and looking around, hung it up on the apple tree. Rolling up my sleeves, I dragged her over to the rubbish hole.

"Put your fingers in your mouth!"

She obeyed, but this did not produce the desired effect.

On the ground near the hole lay several large feathers, possibly belonging to the chicken she had received in payment for the pass. Remembering the ritual of Lucullian banquets, I chose the longest and cleanest feather and made proper use of it.

The feather at last did its job.

I held her around the waist, holding her body over the hole. Her stomach beat away, trembled and shuddered in sudden spasms against my hand. But instead of the usual aversion, I felt only a certain kind of compassion toward this creature.

"Well, feel any better?"

She replied something akin to 'aha' and tried to smile.

I helped her back inside the house – now she seemed far lighter – sat her down on a chair and returned for my jacket. Working the creaking shadoof, I drew some water from the well, washed her, wiped her dry and made her eat a pickled tomato. She kept looking at me and obeyed in silence.

"And now you can go to bed."

She looked at me fearfully – after all these operations her eyes had sobered noticeably – but again she dared not say a word.

I opened the door to another room. There I saw a bright

commode and opposite it an iron single bed. It appeared she lived alone in this house. Although the whole house with its two rooms, entrance hall and small kitchen would easily have fitted into the vestibule of Veronika's bourgeois palace.

I helped Bronia to her bed, removed her dirty shoes and retrieved the stained pillow from under the table.

"Go to sleep. No one will touch you: I'll stand guard."

3

There were pickled tomatoes and bread on the table, and something else covered with a plate, but I was not hungry.

I found two books in the bedroom on the commode. Both were in German by authors unknown to me and were printed in gothic script. I tried to read one of them, but couldn't get past the first sentence. I had to postpone reading until I became proficient in German.

I settled into a cane rocking-chair and pondered the situation.

What if that character didn't turn up at all? How long would I sit here?

I felt certain pangs of conscience: my Quixotic actions were unfair toward elder Karpo and driver Stepan. They were waiting for me to set off home, and were probably worried that I had disappeared.

However, these pangs of conscience mustn't have been very acute, for soon I imagined we were rolling along in the cart, there was no longer any driver, only elder Karpo, who was no longer Karpo, but my grandfather, and instead of arriving home to our house on the cliff, we pulled up outside a large building with columns. And a small girl in white underpants ran out to meet us with the words: 'I see no reason to talk with you on familiar terms', and she showed me her tongue.

Perhaps I had been woken by the noise, but I'm sure that I heard everything while already being awake: the door being flung open, the rattle of the latch, the sound of the violently-opened door hitting the wall, and the thud of heavy steps. I was woken by the impending danger.

I rose from the rocker just as a human figure appeared in the

164

black rectangle of the doorway.

For a minute or so (or perhaps it had only been a tenth of a second) we stood appraising each other.

What could he have seen? Hair worn crim style, a tanned face, an unbuttoned jacket, and underneath it a shirt, also unbuttoned. On studying me further, he would have noticed that the jacket fitted me well, the pants too, and the bristling threads on my knee betrayed a patch.

Meanwhile, the first thing I noticed, for some reason, were his boots, the rifle slung across his shoulder and the city police uniform.

'Perhaps this isn't the fellow?' a fanciful thought flashed through my mind. 'Maybe the chief needs an interpreter, and they've sent this policeman to fetch her?'

His face was in the form of a shoe – his nose joined his forehead almost at right angles, he had thick slobbering lips, pimples or blemishes left from them on his cheeks and forehead, and hands with disproportionately short fingers – this convinced me beyond doubt that he was the man...

And we spoke in unison:

I (in Russian): "What do you want?"

He (in Ukrainian): "Who are you?"

And while I was waiting for my words to have an effect on him (and they had no effect at all), he repeated practically the same words, but more threateningly now:

"Who are you, I asked? What are you doing here? Show me your documents?"

Bowing politely, I introduced myself: "I'm a doctor. I'm curing the young lady of all kinds of loathsome characters, who are pestering her with their canine love..."

"What?! I'll have you... just wait..."

And he (now there really was no doubt that this was the fellow) took a step forward and moved to pull his rifle off his shoulder.

But he wasn't fast enough.

In a flash I was standing before him, eye to eye, and asking softly and sweetly, almost endearingly:

"And you, do you want to live?"

His hand froze on the barrel.

165

He kind of cowered, seeming to grow smaller, and finally mumbled:

"I wasn't going to do anything! I just moved the barrel into a more comfortable position, so it wouldn't dig into my shoulders..."

"So that you don't pain my eyes any longer, grab your barrel and effing piss off. The light's been turned off here. And tell anyone else who's been crawling this way, that the shop is closed now."

He retreated to the door, but there, hiding behind the doorjamb, he recovered some of his impudence. And hissed contemptuously through his teeth:

"So, are you some defender of Yids?"

This wasn't the first time I had had to deal with such characters – in the criminal underworld of the *blatny* they never rose above the rank of pickpocket – they would slobber and swear never to do something again, but as soon as your back was turned, they were ready to toss a brick at you.

But I made a glaring mistake by asking peaceably:

"What makes you think she's Jewish? She's Georgian. I ate shashlik with her uncle in Tiflis."

"Mind no one makes shashlik of you," he uttered, ducking outside and slamming the door behind him so hard that bits of plaster fell to the floor.

I didn't rush out after him only because someone behind me grabbed hold of my sleeve, and something wet touched the palm of my hand. Turning around, I saw Bronia. Barefoot, in her underclothes, she knelt on her knees and snuggled up to my hand, her nose wet with tears.

I had to help her to her feet, sit her on a chair and give her some water...

"Well, I'm going now," I said, finishing tending to her.

She grabbed at my sleeve again and burst into tears:

"He'll be back... Wait here until she returns..."

"Who is 'she'?"

"Sonia..."

Dragging the words out of her one by one, I learnt that Sonia should have been here at five, but would certainly be here any moment now...

Bronia's 'any moment' dragged on for an eternity.

From the bedroom came the girl's even breathing. She was asleep.

I stepped outside for a breath of fresh air, and returned to the room. Semi-dark during the day, it had become bright and well-lit: the mournful setting sun had reached her window through the branches of the apple trees.

A shaft of light struck the untidy table, where apart from the dirty crockery, there were still some pickled tomatoes and bread, and from a pot covered with a plate a chicken drumstick peered enticingly.

I remembered that it was dinner time and slid my chair up to the table, sliced up some bread, and put several tomatoes onto a clean plate. But they weren't to my taste.

Yielding to temptation, I pulled out the piece of roast chicken.

Something flashed past the window and the kitchen door opened without a sound. The golden rays of the setting sun struck the doorway and in their reflection I saw a tall girl enter: she was thin-waisted, with drooping shoulders and radiant golden hair, combed into a 'German doll' hairstyle. Her face and neck were pale pink in colour and against this background of pink her pug nose appeared an unbecoming blot. It was neither too big, nor too ugly, it merely looked unnatural, as if transplanted from another face which it would have suited.

"Another one!" she announced, noticing me. "How many of you bastards keep coming here?! And even gorging yourself on chicken... Slicked up your hair and think you're something! Alright, quick march out of here! Who lied to you that she's Jewish? Won't give the poor girl any peace!"

During her monologue she continued to draw closer, and suddenly, with a swing of her hand, she struck my shock of hair. In reply, I stood up and quite unexpectedly, even for myself, loudly slapped her left cheek.

Noisily gulping air and screaming that she would scratch my eyes out, she jumped up to me to realise her intention. But I grabbed her by the wrists. She leaned over to bite my finger, but I shoved her own hand towards her teeth. She tried to kick me with her foot, but struck a chair and skinned her knee.

Leaving her hands in mine for a minute, she seemed to calm down. Only the movement of her cheeks showed that she was filling her mouth with spittle, preparing to spit in my face.

I was saved by Bronia, who, woken by the crashing of the chair and her friend's screaming, rushed from the bedroom, shouting: "Sonka, stop! Sonka, are you crazy?!"

She rushed to separate us. Taking advantage of the situation, I pushed Sonka away from me, grabbed my cap and dashed outside.

And set off at a quick pace toward the council offices.

When I was some distance away I recognized Sonia's voice. She had run outside and was shouting something after me. I only caught single words, but couldn't make any sense of them and didn't turn around.

The sun was setting and everything was flooded with a bright golden-pink light. The air was heavy with the smell of jasmine and night-scented stocks.

But the fragrant and peaceful evening was unable to assuage my bad mood.

Why had I come to this city? I hadn't landed a job, hadn't passed any messages on to Petro Matviyovych and Vania. And where I needed to act, I acted the incorrectly. I should have punched the character from the council offices in the teeth and sworn at the arrogant Veronika in the coarsest language I knew, and broken a few of the policeman's ribs. But I had done none of this. And everything building up inside of me, brewing, to later break out in a slap which I had given poor Sonia for no reason at all.

As I rounded a corner I almost tripped over a short, stocky policeman who emerged from a gateway. I sensed his searching, hateful gaze upon me.

Perhaps in cities, as was the custom in smaller towns, one needed to greet everyone one came across – both friend and stranger.

To hell with him!

I walked past him, and neither he nor I said a word. Only after I had taken about ten steps, did I suddenly hear: "Stop!"

I turned around without stopping. The policeman was walking after me, holding his rifle at the ready. "Stop! Hands in the air, or I'll shoot!"

I stopped, half turned around, but did not raise my hands:

"Shoot, only not at me...!"

A bullet whizzed past me and I heard the report of the rifle.

But it wasn't the policeman who had stopped me who was shooting. The shot came from the other side of the street. Another policeman was crawling out through a hole in the fence. The same fellow with the boot-like mug whom I had driven out of Bronia's place.

And suddenly I understood Sonia's words, which I had not understood and had not wanted to hear: '...they're watching... another street...!!!' It had been a warning and some good advice.

The spot had been well chosen, so that it would turn out best for them and worst for me: to the left was the solid wall of a shed, over which even Vitaliy Lazarenko[35] couldn't have leapt, to the right stood some character, behind me was another fellow. Some ten steps separated us – far too close to allow me to escape, too far to be able to disarm him.

With no other way out, I raised my hands.

"This the one?" the stocky fellow asked.

"That's him," the Boot replied.

The boys were experienced: the Boot came around from behind and, holding his rifle almost horizontally, placed the barrel against the back of my neck, while the stocky one set about checking my pockets.

A brown temporary passport, a white declaration from the village council, a pocket knife, an indelible pencil and an unused handkerchief – this was the result of his search.

Stepping back toward the gate, where the shed cast no shadows, the stocky fellow read aloud everything in my documents, the first ones I had which were not falsified, which contained my proper name, surname, date and place of birth.

The white declaration confirmed that I was an inhabitant of such and such a village and had to go to the city. It was dated with yesterday's date and applied to today.

"Well, he's no bigwig," he said with a sigh of relief, after finishing reading it.

---

[35] A Soviet acrobat known best for his amazing acrobatic skills.

I was led away along the well-worn brick footpaths of this endless city, with my arms in the air.

At first they tried to make fun of me:

"Oh well, that's good," one of them said. "You'll see a bit of the world. Eighteen Germans have been killed near Chernihiv and we need to find eighteen hundred people to be executed. And there are only seven hundred in prison, and most of those are Gypsies. So you'll help make up the numbers..."

"Don't worry, you won't, be taken away anywhere," the second fellow assured me. "Every region has received an order to hang three people to frighten the populace. You'll be swinging in the wind, drying in the sun. And the rope will go squeak-squeak. And your mother will come and sob: 'Oh, my darling son, my dear one!' And the ravens will answer her: 'Kraa-kraa! How true, old woman!'"

Both of them guffawed.

I said nothing.

The elusive evening light slowly melted away. In the yards, under the trees, along the narrow lanes the twilight grew thicker and smelt of stocks and violets.

Were the village elder and the driver still waiting for me, or had they gone home? Perhaps they had already reached the village and Uncle Karpo was standing shaking his head, spreading his arms apart, telling my mother:

"He went to look for an interpreter. And didn't come back. We thought he might have been home already. But don't worry! He'll be here tomorrow. He's not a small boy, he won't get lost."

And mother would hold back her tears, not knowing who to trust: Karpo or her own intuition, which had prophesied ill that morning.

And on the river grandpa Rybalka and Dmytro Bunchuk were paddling out to set the trammel-nets and exchanged a few sparse words, which echoed all the way to Koshlayi, and they glanced up at the house on the cliff, wondering why I was not at home. Or maybe they weren't, for Dmytro must have heard that we had gone to the city with Uncle Karpo. And grandpa Rybalka, who knew everything before it happened, probably expressed a crafty supposition: 'Must be staying the night with some young

170

interpreter...'

And a pink gilt covered the young bulrushes and the tops of the osier. And the pleasantly warm water became black as tar.

And then the moon would rise, and the white house would be clearly reflected in the water –as if it was standing on the very edge of the cliff.

"Ruff! Ruff!" yapped a mangy ailing dog, dashing from an open gate.

I shuddered all over.

The policemen guffawed:

"He's waging war on Hitler and yet scared of dogs."

The small dog yapped in a human voice and tried to grab at my left trouser leg.

But I couldn't chase it away, because I knew that if I made one inadvertent move, the Boot would sink a bullet between my shoulder blades.

There were no dogs in our village, apart from the accountant's mutt Liutnia, and even it would rub its sides against my leg. There were two or three dogs in Vokhre, but I rarely went there and had become quite unaccustomed to the barking of dogs.

"Sic 'im! Sic 'im!" the Boot called out.

The dog became frightened and ran back to its gate.

The policemen began talking about their police matters, about girls and vodka. Then they grew quiet.

We walked along the winding streets. It was four kilometres from Bronia's place to the council offices, and about two more to the police station. Here and there women peeped out from their gates, trying to tell in the darkness who was being led away.

Occasionally I heard timid remarks:

"They've led someone off..."

"He's not a local..."

4

People say 'he didn't move a finger' and never think that a person can't always move their fingers. I, for instance, couldn't move mine now. My white bloodless fingers hung limply at my side and if one of the policemen had decided to order me to lift my

171

hands again, I wouldn't have been able to carry out his orders.

I was sitting in the office of the police chief, waiting till he decided to focus his attention on me.

My hopes that someone would rescue me had not eventuated: the village elder had obviously gone home. Though I did notice a cart in the council office grounds as we passed them and there was someone standing beside the cart – but it had not been Uncle Karpo.

And there was no one I knew in the police station.

The chief moved around slightly and now, in the light of the kerosine lamp, I could see his face. I almost called out – it was... but who? He reminded me of someone. Not quite Pashka Orlan, not quite Vaska the Gypsy. Though Pashka had white eyebrows and blonde hair, while Vaska was olive-skinned and had brown hair, with a possible admixture of African blood. So it wasn't an individual likeness, but a merely something about his stance, his professional appearance. Yes, a teacher always reminds one of a teacher, and a carter – of a carter. And an *urka* – of an *urka*.

As if in answer to my thoughts he got up from reading a large grey sheet of paper, which the policemen had placed on the table together with my documents, looked at me closely and said unexpectedly:

"Do you know Vaska the Gypsy?"

"If I don't, nobody else does."

"What about Sevka Lukianenko?"

"I don't remember anyone by that name."

"But you and I..."

It was Sevka Lukianenko standing before me. He remembered Vaska and me from the homeless refuge. He had even slept in the same room as us. And since Vaska and I had been the heroes of several reckless escapades – stories continued to circulate about us for a long time after our escape. He had not forgotten about the herrings I had treated him to, when three of us homeless kids – Vaska, myself and some other fellow – had rolled out a barrel of herrings in broad daylight from the workers cooperative store.

I made it clear to him that the third fellow had not been a homeless urchin, but the quiet and obedient Niki – the teacher's son. But I did not bother explaining that it had not been a barrel, only a small keg.

He began to tell me about the boys, girls and teachers we had known...

The past came to life. And at the same time I began to feel pins and needles in my arms and they came back to life.

Our conversation created a lyrical mood – for what can be more lyrical than reminiscences. And I began to tell him about my meeting with Niki – a moment which gave birth to the most interesting year in my whole life. About the blue-eyed Klava, Vaska the Gypsy's wife, the Orlan brothers...

"What about Kolka the Bitch..." Sevka interrupted my account.

I didn't hear the rest of his words, for suddenly my mind was flooded with one of those events which I had firmly and steadfastly tried to forget, using sheer willpower, determined not to revisit it even in my dreams.

I keenly felt as if I was reliving the moment. The refuge's hyena, Kolka the Bitch, pestered me to give him a herring.

"I haven't got any herrings. Get lost!"

He moved away, but said in a threatening tone from a distance:
"I know who you really are!"

And that evening I was called out to see the director. And I remembered the tall thin teacher – what was his name? – who whispered to us in the passage: "Boys, get out of here quick smart, the GPU will be here shortly to pick you all up."

And there on a chair in a corner of the director's office sat frightened Kolka, most probably kept here for a face-to-face confrontation. Or perhaps they had just confused his denunciation with my crime, Vaska and the stolen herrings...

And Vaska never even knew that Ira had previously done time on death row, and if he was still alive, probably still thought that it was all a continuation of the affair with the herrings...

"What's the matter, you asleep?" Sevka Lukianenko's voice jolted me back to reality. "I asked you: who knifed Kolka the Bitch – you or Vaska?"

"Why, did he die? We didn't even know... Vaska jabbed him with a knife."

"And who splashed ink in the director's eyes?"

"He grabbed us by the arms and thought he could hold onto us, so I bashed him on the forehead with a bottle of ink."

"The GPU came looking for you back then. They said you weren't street urchins at all, but kulak children who belonged to a gang, that Vaska had shot a militiaman..."

"The boys told me they'd caught a paratrooper who was pasting up propaganda leaflets. They're lying, the scumbags! They don't drop people like you out of aeroplanes!"

"Of course they're lying. I've been home four months now. At first I lay sick in bed, but then I became so lazy, that I didn't venture anywhere further than Vokhre or Koshlayi. Our place is nice. If you've been through the village, you must have seen the estate on the cliff, surrounded by lindens and pines. You can see it from quite a way off."

"Hold on," Sevka interrupted me again. "Hrytsko Harmash wasn't talking about you, was he, when he said someone had returned home after being executed seven times?"

"Well, seven is a bit of an exaggeration..."

"Obviously not enough for you, you want more. You come to the city and poke your head into a noose straight away. Where did you get this? Did you need to stuff it into your pocket?"

He handed me the large grey sheet of paper lying beside my passport and certificate. It was a cyclostyled proclamation by an underground committee, in the name of the homeland and Stalin, calling on the populace to fight the invader. The sheet had been printed that day, for it contained the names of some of those executed, and promised that the fascist usurpers would be avenged.

"The boys brought me this: said they caught you red-handed, pasting them up on the fences. You're lucky I'm here. Were it anyone else, you would have been packed off to the Gestapo straight away."

"Where's the glue then? Tell them to bring the pot of glue, otherwise the lie won't stick to me... I'm massaging my hands because they're drained of blood," I said in reply to Sevka's gaze. "They marched me for six kilometres with my arms in the air. And then planted this stuff on me. Your boys need their heads bashed in. To teach them who to take vengeance on."

"Vengeance? Vengeance for what?"

"For a certain matter... Because I bundled the younger one, the one with a boot for a muzzle, out of a certain lady's place – and I really regret not having beaten the daylights out of him as well."

"I know who you mean," said Sevka. "Across the river in the orchards there's a solitary house where a dark-haired lass lives. I organised her documents for her and found her a job as an interpreter. And the boys must have found out. I'll have to tell them the shop has been closed... Know what? Let's have a drink!"

After the first glass Sevka returned my papers to me, after the second he made me a present of a confiscated revolver, about which the German leadership had no knowledge; after the third glass we began to feel hot, and Sevka opened a window. We heard two carts rattling along a nearby cobbled street, and I began to recite from Rylsky[36]:

The distant rattle of a cart in the fields.
Who is heading where and why...?

But Sevka interrupted me, and we sat down on the windowsill and launched into an urchin ditty:

He loved to go to the pictures,
And the theatre, and the circus;
While in his empty purse there was
But a large bedraggled hole...

At these words the squat policeman burst into the room, screaming:

"Sevka, there's a kerfuffle here!"

He stopped dead in his tracks, spying our utopian idyll. A slap came from the passage. And hard on his heels there entered a German officer with a high-forehead and greying temples, accompanied by a painted lady with a monumental bust (I immediately guessed that this was Baron von Trippenbach and Leonida Leonivna). They were followed by Sonia, Bronia, the regional chief in his horn-rimmed glasses, the village elder Karpo and Harmash, a policeman from Koshlayi.

In the doorway stood our driver Stepan, and behind him the Boot, bearing the imprint of five fingers on his frightened face.

And then everyone began to speak at once. Herr Baron was accusing, Sevka was justifying himself in a hodgepodge of

---

[36] Maksym Rylsky (1895-1964) was an outstanding 20th century Ukrainian poet.

Ukrainian, Russian and German:

"*Er ist mein besser Freund.* Translate to him, that this is the best *drug* of my youth…"

Village elder Karpo was talking to everyone and to no one in particular:

"We got held up a little at Oleksiy Platonovych's. Then Stepan come's running in, shouting that they've led him away!"

Sonia came right up to me and said rapturously:

"Gee you're a quick one! We've come here to save you from the gallows and you're already drinking vodka here…"

I wanted to say something in reply, but someone offered me another glass, which had to be emptied in a sign of general conciliation. And I must have emptied it.

Because after that night, I can remember only one detail that night: I was standing at the window, Sonia and Bronia at my side, and from somewhere far away, from beyond the river, maybe even from the orchard in which Bronia's house was lost, came a nightingale's warble.

[….]

Lightning Source UK Ltd.
Milton Keynes UK
UKHW052240230123
415808UK00022B/1865